GUNFIGHT AT THE O.K. CORRAL

Nelson C. Nye

Chivers Press
Bath, England • **G.K. Hall & Co.**
Thorndike, Maine USA

Gill Group $22.95   LP
3/01   Nye

This Large Print edition is published by Chivers Press, England, and by G.K. Hall & Co., USA.

Published in 2001 in the U.K. by arrangement with Golden West Literary Agency.

Published in 2001 in the U.S. by arrangement with Golden West Literary Agency.

U.K. Hardcover ISBN 0-7540-4409-2 (Chivers Large Print)
U.K. Softcover   ISBN 0-7540-4410-6 (Camden Large Print)
U.S. Softcover   ISBN 0-7838-9317-5 (Nightingale Series Edition)

The text of this Large Print edition is unabridged.
Other aspects of the book may vary from the original edition.

Set in 16 pt. New Times Roman.

Printed in Great Britain on acid-free paper.

British Library Cataloguing in Publication Data available

Library of Congress Cataloging-in-Publication Data

Nye, Nelson C. (Nelson Coral), 1907–
   Gunfight at the O.K. Corral : novelized by Nelson C. Nye ; based on the screenplay by Leon Uris.
     p.   cm.
   ISBN 0-7838-9317-5 (lg. print : sc : alk. paper)
   I. Uris, Leon, 1924– II. Title.
   PS3527.Y33 G8 2001
   813'.54—dc21   00–047184

PART ONE
FORT GRIFFIN

CHAPTER ONE

This was buffalo country. All that vast stretch of uncharted prairie west of the river was stomping ground for uncounted thousands of the shaggy-shouldered animals, worth from four to five dollars a hide in the aggregate, and the hunters and their crews were coming in from all over. In the town Conrad's store was taking in $4,000 a day—this was in the time when a dollar was a dollar—and the bulk of this trade done on guns, lead and powder. Hides were piled everywhere, bloody feasts for the flies. It took a strong stomach to live with that smell.

Fort Griffin on the Clear Fork of the Brazos was booming. 'The Flat' itself, as the town was called, had three inexhaustible sources of revenue: the hide men, the troopers, and the free-spending drovers who rode in from the trail herds to 'see the elephant jump to the moon.' Treeing the town, this sport was called later. The merchants hadn't yet become fed up with it. Gamblers waxed fat, and the liquor peddlers likewise. Pimps and their whores were thicker than fleas, and fourteen establishments catered to thirsts. Many of these employed 'girls' in addition to derringer-packing tinhorns to help separate the fools from their money.

The post, established in 1867 by Lieutenant Colonel S.D. Sturgis, topped a mild rise known as 'Government Hill,' with the houses of ranchmen and other settlers strung about it like a brood of chickens. Nearby was a village of friendly Tonkawa Indians, many of whom acted as guides and scouts for the constant comings and goings of the military. Some of the Tonks' Women also found employment about the post and in the wild town as well. Bugle calls regulated the round of activities: reveille at daybreak, stables shortly after, sick call at 6:45, breakfast 7:00, drill 7:30, recall 8:30, guard mount 9:30, water call 11:15, orderlies 11:45, recall from fatigue at 12:00 sharp, and so on, these calls permeating and having a considerable influence upon all life within hearing.

It was just after orderly call, with the brassy notes still quivering in the glittering sun-flushed air, when three horsebackers clothed in the garb of range hands came in sight of the town on a bluff across the river and hauled up against the haze-cushioned blue like a circling of vultures to give the place a sharp-eyed scanning.

This was Ed Bailey with his right and left bower, Alby and Rick, three of a kind, dark against the sweeping lift of the sky, not yet identifiable above the sun-yellowed grass, but in some singular fashion synonymous with trouble. It was a feeling oozing out of the way

4

they sat their saddles, dark faces scrinched and unblinking, no loose talk or laughter.

Having had his look, Bailey lifted the reins and heeled his bronc into a surly canter. The three passed the cemetery, turned into the fetlock-deep dust of the road and came jogging on, eyes narrowed beneath the cuffed brims of their hats.

It wasn't much of a town, even for the frontier, being more a helter-skelter conglomeration of jerrybuilt shacks whipped out of green lumber which had never known paint and was already warped and grotesquely twisted at every joint and hit-or-miss angle. Bailey eyed the freight office, his glance passing over a mired-down wagon that had been there for three weeks and never dug out though the mud which had trapped it was now stiff as baked bricks. He saw the three wagons crammed high with stinking hides creaking in from the west, and the government supply train—crawling specks in the distance. His angry glance picked up the cavalry detail, with its two Tonk scouts, jogging in from the north. No trifling bit of activity on that street escaped his notice. He showed a hard and sullen face darkly burned by the sun and heavily stubbled. Two big pistols in tied-down holsters joggled at his hips, and the stock of a Spencer rifle stuck out of the scabbard under his left leg. Here was no kind of man to slap your hip and yell boo! at. Danger was reflected in every crease and dust-grimed wrinkle.

They turned into the street, Bailey slightly in front, Alby and Rick with their horses' noses just back of his saddle skirts, one at either side. These two looked what they were, just a pair of tough hands, paid gunslingers, and none too happy to be where they were.

Several lounging men on the roundabout porches silently eyed them as the trio rode past the Astor Hotel. Bailey twisted his head and gave the place a hot stare. Two loafers playing checkers on its verandah stopped their game to scan the riders with knowing looks, and a buxom woman with a prominent nose came into the open doorway to glare and turn quickly back into the lobby.

The three riders, reining up across from the hotel, stepped out of their saddles in front of John Shanssey's Saloon & Gambling Hall. Four men, coming out, stopped cold to regard them with shocked and clearly watchful eyes. A man with a deputy's star on his vest, coming out of an alley, very nearly ran into them, then pulled back for a cold prickling instant of silence. Bailey snorted and pushed through the batwings, his two dogs at his heels. The deputy, Wayne, tramped hurriedly off down the street, dust spurting up in little bursts behind his boots.

The inside of Shanssey's place resembled most others of its kind. Lighted with hanging Rochester lamps whose wicks were only

6

snuffed for refueling, it was perhaps a little more ornate than its competitors and had the added distinction of offering more floorspace and, it was said, a greater variety of feminine 'pulchritude.' There were not many customers on hand when Bailey came in with his gunhands, but these were quick to note the look on his face and step back to leave ample room at the bar.

The sleeve-gartered, bald-headed barkeep made haste to move up.

'Whisky,' Bailey said. 'An' leave the bottle.'

John Shanssey, every inch a dandy in frock coat and flowered waistcoat, his stomach crossed with a cable of gold watch chain, was ensconced in a rear booth feeding his face. He got up, spotting Bailey. He put a cigar in his mouth, flicked a match into flame, sent out a few puffs of smoke that ballooned ceilingward like signals, and came down the mahogany. 'You back again, Ed?'

Bailey said, 'Where's Holliday?'

'Expect he's probably over to the hotel. He laid a bet you'd show. You better think this over, Ed—'

'Get him word I'm waitin' for him.'

Shanssey looked at him coldly. 'All you'll do with a play like that is get yourself planted. You better—'

'Just stick with your watered-down rotgut and leave shootin' business to them as understands it. No sonofabitch is goin' to cut

7

down my brother an' get away with it.'

'Your brother came in here stinking drunk. He was spoiling for a fight, Ed. He made a passel of talk not many gents would take. Doc let it roll off'n him. Then your brother went for his gun.'

'You keep out of this, Shanssey. I know what I'm doin'.'

'Well,' Shanssey said, 'it's your hide, Ed. If you're bound for a burying I guess he'll oblige you.'

Bailey, snatching the bottle from the bar, shoved past. Shanssey said over his shoulder, 'Leave your guns with the barkeep if you aim to drink here.'

Bailey wheeled around as though he'd been hit by a wasp. His men swapped glances. Bailey finally nodded.

'Okay.' All three laid their unbuckled belts on the bar. They went back to a table near the rear and sat down where they could watch the batwings.

*   *   *

Upstairs in the hotel, in a shade-drawn shadowed room, a knifeblade flashed and thunked point-first into a wall. Across a rumpled bed a gangling, pasty-faced, wire-thin man slaunched in a hard-bottomed chair, rocking it forward and back on its spindling hind legs. On a stand beside him stood a half-filled bottle of whisky, an empty tumbler and a dozen throwing knives, their sharp blades glinting in the uncertain light. The large-breasted woman with the prominent nose—the one who had watched Bailey & Company ride past the hotel—had her face to the curtain edge, angrily watching the street. She said, 'You haven't got a chance, Doc. He brought a pair of hardcases in with him, Alby and some other whey-faced rat. You step out on that street—' The consumptive dentist who called himself Holliday chunked another knife beside the first one in the wall. He poured the tumbler half full of whisky, tossed back his head and downed the whole drink in one gulp.

'Jesus, honey,' Big Nose Kate said, 'let's quit this town while we've still got the chance. This whole goddam place, includin' that cold-footed marshal, is layin' for you!'

Doc, ignoring her, bedded another blade.

'Right or wrong, your neck's due for stretchin' if you kill another man. Don't you understand?' she cried, desperate. 'Goddam it, you ain't even listenin'!'

'Now, Kate,' Doc said, 'Mr. Bailey's come all the way from Fort Worth for this business. Wouldn't be polite for me to light a shuck now. You wouldn't want me to disappoint him now, would you?'

'Spare me that stinkin' Southern gentleman routine. I'm thinkin' about your neck, not your face.'

Holliday grinned. 'Purely a case of ethics, my dear. Of course, I know you don't know much about ethics—'

'You always got to treat me like I'm dirt under your feet?'

'Well—' Doc said, and heaved another knife. 'Ain't you?'

'Sometimes, by God,' Kate said, looking plumb driven, 'I think I ort to poison you! Lemme tell you somethin', Doc. Them fancy duds and that smart talk don't make you out no gentleman to me. I know what's underneath them things an' don't you never ferget it! Maybe I'm dirt, but there's good women too—girls you ain't fit to be around even.'

Doc yawned. 'That's debatable.' But he was irritated, too. He snapped another blade into the wall with a force that buried almost half its length.

Kate's lips twisted scornfully. 'Ain't this about the stage where you tell me about your family's aristocratic Georgia plantation and all your fine proud friends an' the wenches—'

'One of these days I'm like to strangle you, Kate.' He grinned beneath his debonair mustache but there was nothing pleasant about it. He looked deadly as a rattler, tail up and warnings posted. After a moment he turned away from her and slammed another blade into the wall. He was touchy about his family.

10

But Kate couldn't let it alone. 'Your folks must've scraped the barrel after the war to put you through that tooth-yanker's school. You're a real credit to 'em. They'd be sure-enough proud to—'

A knife quit Doc's hand and drove into the boards about an inch from Kate's head. She blinked and winced, stunned. Yanking the steel from the wall she rushed wildly at him, furiously lunging, mad enough to disembowel him.

Doc quit the chair in one bound and grabbed her. She was a chunky, husky woman who knew every trick of barroom brawling but she was no match for Doc. He twisted her knife hand behind her, shoved it up her back, not giving a damn whether he broke it or not. With his free hand twisted into her high-piled hair he forced her head back, his eyes as hard as stones.

'You're hurtin' me!' Kate gasped.

'Let go of that knife.'

She tried to struggle, to jerk loose of him. Doc put on more pressure, bringing her almost to her knees. The knife got away from her. She slumped panting against him. 'Ah, lover,' she moaned, 'let's don't fight.'

Doc, stepping back, said colder than frogs' legs, 'Don't ever mention my family again.'

He straightened his string tie and the hang of his coat, wiping his hands irascibly on the skirts of it. Kate, nervously eyeing him, said,

'God, you sure are jumpy today, honey. Look—why don't you forget this guy, Bailey? Let's you an' me go off someplace and have a little fun. Maybe we can do something about that cough . . . Sounds to me like it's gettin' worse.'

'Your concern for my health deeply touches me,' Holliday said with his lip twisting down in a sneer.

She flung her arms about his neck. 'You know how I feel about you.' She shoved the fullness of her breasts against him, grinding her hips, but the man wasn't interested. 'I know,' he said nastily, 'exactly how you feel.'

Kate looked at him, big-eyed, a little breathless. 'I don't know what I'd do if anything was to happen to you.'

The natty killer pulled her arms from around his neck, threw her off, and stepped distastefully back. 'Worrying about your meal ticket, are you?'

Kate's chin came up, and there was plenty of it. 'That's a hell of a thing to say to me. I've been good to you, Doc. It's about time you thought a little bit about me.'

He looked at her slanchways, and grinned thinly. 'Well—I suppose the *girls* would be happy to regain a charter member.'

Kate slapped his face, her own turning ugly with the fury surging through her. Heaping insult on injury that nasty smirk appeared again around Holliday's mouth and in the cut of his stare. His hand half raised as though to return the blow, but she did not cringe and he finally dropped it. Then he reached out, patting her rouged cheek and smiling. 'Get over to Shanssey's. Tell him I'll be around later, soon's I work some of the kinks out of my system.'

'*Please* don't go there!'

'Do what I tell you.' Holliday scowled and Kate, defeated, said bitterly, 'I've got to have some money.'

Doc dug a bill from his wallet and held it out without comment. Kate took it, tucked it into the crevice between billowy breasts and stomped from the room like a wet-footed cat. Doc, laughing, poured himself another generous slug and walked over to the mirror, patting down his hair. He was a handsome man by any standard, handsome despite his almost constant dissipation and the ravages of tuberculosis. He took no care at all of himself, aside from his personal appearance, about which he was inordinately vain and upon which he focussed a most fastidious attention. He was invariably groomed to the nines. He stood for a few moments poking at his mustache. Then he opened a watch which he took from the lower right-hand pocket of his magnificent vest.

He stood lost in thought, staring at a picture that was just inside the cover. This showed an attractive woman and a man in Confederate uniform. Snapping the cover closed he stared a further moment at an engraved inscription which read: *To our beloved son, Doctor John Holliday.*

Doc took another frowning look into the mirror past the whisky glass, a cartridge belt and holstered pistol and the hilts of the knives he'd driven into the wall. He could not seem to stand the sight of the dough-colored face reflected back at him. A violent seizure of coughing came over him.

When this was finally quelled, he scrubbed the blood from his lips and looked again at the face, flushed now, mouth twitching.

Doctor John Holliday.

'You sonofabitch!' he shouted, and sent the watch crashing into the mirror. The flash of gold bounded back from the broken shards of glass, fell to the boards of the floor and rolled. Doc, kneeling contritely, picked the watch up, gently cradling it in shaking fingers. His eyes were watery, his white teeth clenched . . .

CHAPTER TWO

In a land where the laws, and the order these were fondly propounded to establish, were most frequently the subject of inordinate belly laughs or caustic comment, one man at least was rumored to take them with deadly seriousness and was, in consequence, pretty

14

thoroughly disliked by the element which provided most of the noise in that locality. This man, six feet tall and weighing a hundred and fifty without his boots and shell belt, was a blue-eyed blond. The whip of the wind and the blaze of the sun had baked many lines in his face, particularly about the eyes, and the cold-jawed mouth almost hidden behind the luxuriant bristles of an elegant jowls-sweeping handlebar mustache.

The name of this fellow was Wyatt Earp.

In the dust and bright glare of that windy afternoon when the trail of Dave Rudabaugh fetched Wyatt into Fort Griffin he was twenty-nine years old, veteran of many things and places. He'd known Kansas and Nebraska when Omaha and K.C. were helltearing border towns. As a freighter he'd driven bull teams on the Overland and Santa Fe trails. He'd hunted buffalo and Injuns and been a professional gambler. He'd policed Wichita when that place was considered one of the wildest towns on the 'Circuit' and knew most of the rougher toughs of the time through firsthand or, at least, a sort of nodding acquaintance. Some of them he knew more thoroughly than their mothers, for he had heard the owl hoot and the owl had heard him. Currently employed by the Atcheson, Topeka and the Santa Fe he was, in the freewheeling parlance of the day, a railroad dick.

Life on the Flat hardly got under way,

generally speaking, before the middle of any evening. Only a few Yankee shopkeepers hunting transient customers were earlier astir; the Big Guns seldom strolled into view before the fashionable hour of chimney smoke and supper preparations. It was scarcely three o'clock now. Wyatt had dawdled deliberately these last few miles, aiming to reach Griffin in time for a look around before his man should hear any whisper of his advent.

Turning his mount with one toe toward a hitching rail he called to the hostler at the stable across the street: 'Hey!'

The old man limped over, scrubbing at his neck with a grimy once-red bandanna. Wyatt, stepping stiffly out of the saddle, said, 'See that this horse gets bedded down, then fetch my saddlebags over to the hotel.'

The man commenced to bristle; then, taking a more careful note of this stranger's hard stare, he mumbled, 'Yessir.'

Inside the Marshal's Office, into which Earp tramped with the heaviness of a man who'd been long off the ground, Cotton Wilson, the incumbent star-packer and a reluctant acquaintance of Wyatt's from away back, looked up with a grunt from his rifle cleaning and scowled. He'd about as soon have tangled with the Old Itch himself as to see Wyatt Earp stepping into his bailiwick. There'd been a time when Cotton Wilson was a hard man with a pistol, but this was far in the past—on the very fringe of memory. He had a good thing here and wasn't minded to turn loose of it.

'Howdy, Wyatt,' he finally growled.

'Hello yourself. Been a long time, Cotton.'

Cotton reluctantly put out a hand, involuntarily wincing as Earp vigorously shook it. Getting up, the marshal replaced his rifle in the gunrack, turning back with a wary slanchways stare. Wyatt, yawning and stretching, wearily plopped down into a chair. 'By God, I'm plain wore out. Hope you've scraped up some good news for me . . . Got my message, didn't you?'

Wilson, nervous, reluctantly nodded. He studied his gnarled old hands, wheezing and glowering.

'Well? Speak out. Didn't he show?'

'You're talkin' about Ike Clanton, I reckon.' When Wyatt just stared, Wilson said, desperate, 'He come through here three days ago, headin' east. Ringo was with him.'

'Headin' east? Rode through . . . Didn't you get my wire?'

' 'Course I got it. Don't lookit me like that. Jesus Christ, I'm only one man!'

Still Wyatt stared. The marshal squirmed. Wyatt, getting up, said, 'Why didn't you hold him?'

'I got no quarrel with Ike,' Wilson flared. 'Ain't nothin' round here I could hold him *for*!'

'What do you call 'nothing'? There's twenty charges hangin' over that ruffian!' The Santa

17

Fe's man looked both disgusted and outraged. 'Rudabaugh's trail was already cooled off when they put me on it, but I cut Ike's tracks when the grass hadn't hardly sprung back from his passin'. He was headed this way—that's why I sent you that wire.'

He looked like for two cents he would work Wilson over. 'I played this whole deal so's he'd be forced into Griffin. Seemed like if there was one star in Texas I could depend on to stop him, you'd be the man.'

'Now don't go rilin' yourself into no lather,' Wilson said, raising his voice some. 'I got t' walk a pretty tight line in this place. Clanton had friends here—'

'I never heard tell of you duckin' a fight before.'

'I—well—we just got a different way of runnin' things now. Politics is gettin' so's a man can't hardly spit, half the time, without finding himself backed into some corner. Goddam it,' Wilson said, warming up to this subject, but the Santa Fe's man waved his bluster away.

'This is Wyatt Earp you're a-talking to, Cotton. Ten years ago I watched you walk singlehanded into that saloon back in Oklahoma City and drop three of the fastest pistoleers that ever whacked leather. What's the matter with you, man?'

Wilson stepped around his desk and slumped into the chair like a sack of burst oats.

18

'I know it, but that was ten years ago. I'm gettin' old, Wyatt.'

'Is that what you call it?' Earp shook his head. 'If any man would of told me Cotton Wilson was going to turn yaller I'd have called him a dadburned hypothecatin' liar.'

He went over and settled a hip on the corner of Wilson's desk.

The red-faced marshal said, 'You've got no call to make a crack like that. You don't know what I'm up against. You don't know the misery I got in my back, boy. There's times I ain't got no hand for it at all. Things ain't like they used t' be. Marshalin' ain't the same no more—it's all politickin' now. It's who you know an' how you set with 'em. I've bucked some of the toughest gangs in the West—'

'Then whyn't you stop Ike Clanton an' Ringo? If you can't handle fellers like them any more whyn't you peel off that tin?'

'Goddam it,' Wilson snarled, 'I told you! My hands is tied. I can't cross up them boys. I got too many irons in the fire to—' He chopped the rest off, badly shaken, watching Wyatt like a mouse would a cat with his eyes rolled up until only the whites showed between his scrinched lids.

He blew out an exasperated breath through the yellowed stumps of tobacco-stained teeth. 'I been a lawman now for better'n twenty-five years. What else could I do? I've worked more hellholes than you'll ever see! An' what have I got to show for it? A twelve-dollar-a-month room in the ass-end of a cruddy boardin' house, an' this goddam star!' He said with a squeal of indignation, 'You think I *like* endin' up in a place like this? I've reached the end of the line, same as you're goin' to some day. I'm gettin' mine now any way that I can!'

Wyatt shut his mouth on the things that were struggling inside of him for utterance. He walked out of the place without again looking at the congested face of a man he had once admired and called friend.

*   *   *

The air inside of Shanssey's saloon was tight and piled deep with the threat of an explosion. Every eye in the place was fixed either openly or guardedly on the glowering Bailey and his two tough hands. Ed Bailey, flushed and sweating, bolstered his nerve with another stiff slug from the bottle, but his shaking hand spilled half of it on his chin. He could feel the eyes, and the contempt, skepticism and speculation back of them. It rasped against him like a clawing of nettles. Damn the whole stinking push! His eyes flared back at them, red-rimmed from his riding and the whisky inside him. Everywhere he looked the frozen faces gazed back at him, troopers and bar girls, hunters, gamblers, macs and aproned bartenders, all of them watching in avid

20

expectation. The bottle was nearly empty; he found it hard to focus his attention but he wasn't forgetting what he'd come here for.

'Where is that yellow-livered skunk?' he snarled.

Rick, his left bower, said, muttering it, 'Take it easy, Ed. This whole crowd's in it with him. They're settin' it up to git you riled.' And Bailey's other hand said, 'You better lay off that bottle, boss.'

Down the bar about twenty steps Shanssey had his head tipped, talking into the ear of the head barkeep. Now the apron nodded. He said back of his hand, 'What's keepin' Doc anyway?'

Shanssey grinned. 'Doc's figuring to let him dangle a while.'

Cotton Williams came in with his chief deputy, Wayne, and two others armed with shotguns. These last two posted themselves beside the green-painted batwings, hats low over eyes that were narrowly alert for the first sign of trouble.

At his table Bailey slung the empty bottle into a corner, not much caring if he hit anyone or not. 'Let's hev some decent whisky here!'

In the archway over by the grab-and-stomp part of Shanssey's establishment just beyond the free lunch a bevy of girls in rather scanty attire made bright splotches of color as they stood in a huddle, peering into the saloon. Beyond them, under the balcony overhang,

Kate of the prominent nose sat as though she was held by fiddlestrings at a glass-ringed table in the silent company of another soiled dove. Kate's white-knuckled, garishly beringed and overplump fingers nervously twisted a handkerchief that looked damp with handling, but no damper than her cheeks behind the rouge and rice powder. She wasn't a bad-looking dame if you didn't mind that nose or her too-ready willingness to meet ardent males somewhat more than halfway.

Rumors concerning her were rife in the town. It was said she was a girl Doc had married and discarded after snatching her out of a St. Louis finishing school. She habitually packed a gun, and could use it. She did not wear it in sight but it was always about her somewhere whenever she had occasion to resort to it. Some of the more malicious minded claimed she was a whore by preference, ready to peel off her clothes at the lift of an eyebrow, but she lived where she pleased and paid tribute to no one. She was equally at home on the plains or in town; she was as self-sufficient and as fearless, as fiery-tempered as Doc.

She'd been hanging around Shanssey's place for several months. Doc had been dealing cards there. They saw quite a bit of each other although it was a generally accepted fact that Shanssey himself was paying most of her bills. Doc had been here two months and gave every evidence of regarding himself as a more or less permanent part of the menage. He had no regard for the law whatever and Wilson left him strictly alone.

Kate lifted her half-filled glass and abruptly drained it.

The batwings flapped back and Wyatt Earp stepped into the barroom. A kind of visible relief ran over the place, some of those nearer faces relaxing visibly as, clean-shaven below his yellow sweeping mustache and wearing fresh linen underneath his black vest, he went past Cotton Wilson as though the marshal wasn't there. The whole feel of the place turned easier as a number of the men and even a couple of the unattached girls gathered about him as he stepped up to the bar.

The girl beside Kate got out of her chair and started uncertainly across the dance floor. Kate grabbed her wrist.

'Who's that they're making all that fuss about?'

'Wyatt Earp.'

'You mean the railroad dick? Is that who he is? What's he doing here?'

The girl twisted loose. She went into the saloon, pushed into those around Earp. 'Hi, Wyatt. Bet you don't remember me.'

'Wichita,' Earp said with a grin. 'Sadie's dancehall. How could I forget?'

'See you later?'

'I'll probably be around,' the detective said,

eyes twinkling.

He winked at the girl as several others pushed up to him. John Shanssey elbowed into the circle, grabbed Wyatt's arm and, drawing him away from his admirers, led him into a semi-separated booth at the rear of the room.

Pumping Wyatt's fist, he said, 'You old son of a gun! Whyn't you let us know you was figurin' to ride in?'

'Good to see you, John. Matter of fact, I came here on business.'

Some of the bunch the saloonkeeper had dragged Wyatt away from had followed them all the way back to the booth. As Earp doubled into a seat at the table Shanssey threw out his hands as though to push them away. 'Look, boys, give us a break.' He partially hid his annoyance behind a quick smile. 'I'll turn the famous man over to you later.' He said to Wyatt, 'You eaten yet?'

'No.' The detective watched the others drift reluctantly away. 'Seems like I'm gettin' to be a marked man.'

'Price of fame,' Shanssey chuckled. He caught the glance of a passing waiter. 'You've sure as hell come quite a piece since Cheyenne. Everybody, I guess, has heard of you now. Ellsworth, Wichita, Dodge . . .' He shook his bead. 'Never had you pegged for a lawman, Wyatt. Seemed to me you was always pretty reckless and wild.'

'Still am, some would tell you. In those

24

days,' Wyatt said, referring to the crossing of their trails in '67, 'I figured the world was my oyster. Not so sure of it now.' He put his elbows on the table, thinking back to Cheyenne of ten years ago. Shanssey, a pugilist then, had fancied himself ready to take on Mike Donovan, the Champ. Wyatt had refereed the fight. Shanssey had been so thoroughly drubbed he had never gone into a ring again.

'Guess I never really figured myself for a lawman,' Earp said. 'I just sort of drifted into it. I was standin' in a real bind one day when somebody handed me a star and sixshooter. I haven't been able to get rid of either one.'

The waiter came up. 'Fix a prime steak up for Mr. Earp,' Shanssey said, 'and fetch a bottle of the best from my personal stock.'

'Coffee'll do,' Wyatt said as the man departed.

'You gone temperance?'

'Not really.' Wyatt frowned. 'I've just found that drinkin' and packing a gun don't go so well together. Never seen a drunk yet that could hit the side of a barn.'

Shanssey regarded him thoughtfully. 'You take that badge pretty serious, don't you?'

'I've got to,' Wyatt nodded. 'My life depends on it.'

'How's your brothers?'

'They're gettin' along. Scattered all over the country. Virgil and Morgan are married, you

25

know—though I must say none of us appear to have settled down too well. Guess the Earps ain't the kind to put down many roots.' His eyes focussed keenly on Shanssey's face. 'John, I ain't much of a hand for sayin' so, but I could use a little help.'

Shanssey fired up a stogie. 'Anything I can do.'

'Ike Clanton an' Ringo rode through here three days ago. I went to some trouble to make sure they would, and wired Cotton Wilson to hold them. What's the matter with that feller?'

'He's not the same man we used to know. You see that bar?'

Wyatt's glance drifted barward. He nodded.

'Every one of those boys behind the mahogany is gunfighters. Only way I can keep order. I hate to say it, but I can't help you. I don't know a thing about—say, wait. Let me think.' He snapped his fingers. 'Doc Holliday set into a game with that pair. He might have heard something.'

Over at Ed Bailey's table a clatter went up. The man's mean eyes flicked about him impatiently. 'If that two-by-four bastard,' he said loudly, 'ain't here in twenty minutes I'm goin' after him!'

'That Ed Bailey?' Wyatt asked.

Shanssey nodded. 'Poor damn fool's just askin' to get planted. Doc killed his brother, but there again the guy was begging for it. Mean drunk he was. Cheated at cards, tried to

26

put it on Doc an' yanked his smoke pole.' Shanssey rolled the Long Nine across his teeth. 'You ever met Holliday?'

'Briefly. Once. He was tooth pullin' then. Wonder what turned him into a gunslinger?'

'Never heard. He ain't one to talk about his past. I've yet to see him pick a fight. Far as that goes he don't seem to have to; trouble just naturally gravitates towards him. Bailey's the third man he's killed in the Flat. Gotten so every would-be pistol pusher in the Territory seems to want the name of havin' put him under. You know how it is when a man gets a rep.'

Wyatt nodded soberly. 'I certainly do.'

Shanssey said, 'I've got Doc figured for a mighty short life. Never seen a place so against a man as this one is. Even if Doc fixes this one's clock—mean even if he come out of the smoke—the crowd'll lynch him this time sure. He ain't got a real friend in this camp.'

Wyatt said, 'Where can I find him? If you think there's a chance he might have heard something—'

'He's got a room at the hotel.'

Wyatt got up. 'Keep the steak warm.'

Shanssey smiled. 'You wouldn't be missing too much. It's plain Texas longhorn.'

Wyatt moved past Bailey's table. The man was opening a fresh bottle.

*　　　*　　　*

27

In the Hotel Astor dining room Doc, at dinner, was just setting down a glass. As usual, the gambling dentist was immaculately clad. The big room was about deserted. His dinner finished, Doc pushed back the grease-smeared dishes and began to lay out a hand of solitaire. He moved a few cards, sat a while in concentration. Moving the jack of spades off a turned-down stack, he looked up to see Earp standing over the table.

'Mr. Holliday, I believe,' Wyatt said.

Doc said nothing, just kept moving the cards. Pulling out a chair Wyatt sat down across from him. Doc, without raising his head, said sarcastically, 'Make yourself right at home.'

Wyatt, ignoring his tone, leaned forward. 'Don't know if you remember me.'

'Wyatt Earp,' Doc said. 'I pulled one of your bicuspids ten years ago. If I'd known when I had you in that chair—'

'Understand you've taken up a new occupation. You were a pretty fair dentist.'

'Patients couldn't stand my coughing in their faces.'

He kept on moving the cards. Wyatt reached over to shift a queen for him. Doc grabbed his wrist. 'The name of this game is solitaire, mister.'

Wyatt settled back, grinning patiently.

'Mr. Earp, I'm busy.'

'I'm huntin' information.'

'Hunt somewhere else.'

Wyatt said expansively, 'Let's say I'm in a position to do a little horse trading.'

'Not interested in horses.'

'I think you'll be interested in what I've got to tell you.'

'You couldn't know a thing it would be worth my while to listen to.'

'Don't bet too heavy on it.' Wyatt said, smiling, 'What would you say if I was to tell you Ed Bailey's got a lady's gun hidden in his bootleg?'

'Left or right?'

'Left.'

'I'd say that was good information. Happens Bailey's left-handed.'

Once again Wyatt leaned forward. 'Ike Clanton an' Ringo rode through here three days ago. You know which way they were heading?'

'Beats me,' Doc said.

'Thought we were tradin' information?'

'I didn't make any deals.'

'You probably know where they went, or where they were figurin' to go.'

'You're playing hell with my game.'

Wyatt, glaring at Doc, got stiffly out of his chair. 'You've got no use for the law at all, eh?'

'I'm not hugging and kissing it. Last year, in case you don't know, your fine brother Morgan ran me out of Deadwood. Impounded

29

ten thousand dollars of my money. I should like that?'

'I should be blamed for it?'

'You got brothers wearing tin all over the goddam country.'

'Perhaps I'll run into you again,' Wyatt remarked thoughtfully.

Doc, unperturbed, went on shifting his cards.

CHAPTER THREE

Wyatt, coming back into the saloon, was met by Shanssey. One glance at Wyatt's face seemed to give him the whole story. 'Wasn't talking, eh?'

'Hell with it. I'm headin' back to Dodge City.'

'Too bad,' Shanssey said. What he said then was just like putting the old X straight down on Doc's character. He said, 'You know, he's in my debt for a few things. I believe he'd help you out if I was to ask him.'

Wyatt shrugged it away. 'Ringo and Clanton are probably headed for Tombstone. Ike's old man has a big spread there.'

'Isn't your brother Virgil the marshal at Tombstone?'

'Last I heard, he was. I'm gettin' off a wire to him to keep his eyes skinned for them.'

'Doc say when he's coming over here?'

'What he said you could put in your eye and never feel it.'

Shanssey sighed. 'I sure wish this night was done with.'

*   *   *

Doc, over at the Astor after Wyatt had left, played another couple of cards and tossed in the deck. He poured himself a stiff drink and downed it, wiped his mouth and got out of the chair. Heading for the lobby he put on his hat and stopped by a mirror to adjust his string tie and straighten his coat.

There was no one in the lobby except the bored clerk.

'Oh, Mr. Holliday,' the man said. 'Would you care to settle up your bill? What I mean is—ah—we didn't know whether you'd be checking out or not.'

Doc gave him a hard stare. 'If I do you'll be the first to hear about it. I'm not in the habit of running out on my debts.'

He stepped out on the porch, stood there a few moments gazing across the road at Shanssey's. Perhaps he was thinking about Earp, a little jealous of the man's high standing in the country. Whatever his reflections were they obviously gave him no pleasure, but he did not miss seeing the pair of shapes that came out of the cottonwood's

31

shadows to dart with some furtiveness into the saloon. A smirk tugged at Doc's lips. Whistling softly he moved down onto the walk and, finally, striking off through the dust, he crossed over. While he was still some steps away from the batwings, Shanssey came out and intercepted him.

Shanssey wasted no words. 'You're walking straight into trouble if you go into my place. If Bailey don't get you Cotton Wilson will. You'd be smart to pull your freight while—'

Doc, brushing past him, headed for the doors.

Shanssey said disgustedly, 'You tired of livin', Doc?'

Doc paid him no attention at all. He pushed through the half-leafs and heard the place go still as the news of his presence ran like a wind through the chip clatter and gab. A lane, like magic, opened up between Holliday and Bailey's table. Wyatt, standing a few feet from Cotton Wilson, marveled at the stillness that was, in its way, a kind of tribute to Doc's prowess as a corpsemaker. Shanssey trailed the gambler in. Not once, so far, had the consumptive dentist looked at the man who had come here to bury him.

Cotton Wilson said, 'Wait a minute, Doc. Check in that gun. We don't want no trouble in here.'

Doc, considering the marshal, appraising his determination, finally walled over to him, unbuttoning his coat. Smiling thinly, he pulled it open. There was no gun belt and no gun. He gave Wilson a sour grin and, whistling through his teeth, stepped nonchalantly up to the bar, halting about a yard from Bailey's table. People standing around there scattered. Not by even a lift of the eyebrows did Holliday acknowledge Bailey's presence. Turning his back on the man, he propped a foot on the rail and held up two fingers. The nearest apron set a bottle in motion.

Wyatt shook his head. 'He's got guts, all right.' Shanssey, somewhat tight about the mouth, nodded silently. Cotton Wilson continued to watch Doc edgily, a half-opened hand beside his gunbutt. Kate stepped out of the archway, coming a few steps into the room.

Ed Bailey's hands nervously drummed the table top. Sweat put a greasy shine along his jowls.

Doc held up three fingers and the barkeep poured. He must have been as tightly wound as Bailey but he put every drop of the drink inside the glass. Doc was watching Bailey in the back bar mirror.

Now he said to the barkeep in a voice that carried plainly to the ends of the room, 'I understand there's a gentleman here from Ft. Worth, but I don't observe any gentleman—aside from myself.' He tried the whisky for flavor, even passed the glass back and forth beneath his nose. 'This fellow should have

33

taught his brother the difference between Hoyle and a deck of marked cards.' While the people standing about visibly held their collective breaths, Doc said to the barkeep in the way of one sport confiding in another, 'If anyone should happen to lay eyes on this ranny, kindly pass the word along I'll be waiting at Boot Hill. I'm referring to this son of a yellow bellied sow.'

Bailey staggered to his feet, upending the table. Doc could see every move the fellow made in the mirror. As Bailey bent grotesquely to jerk the pistol from his boot leg Doc dexterously produced a knife from somewhere adjacent to his collar and, abruptly spinning about, caught Bailey in the act of leveling his sixshooter. There was a glint of streaking steel. The gun drove a slug through the tin of the ceiling and Bailey, staggering back, collapsed and doubled over the reddening hilt of the bedded blade.

Alby and Rick, Bailey's hired toughs, started for Doc and were stopped in their tracks by the rock-steady focus of two pistols in the hands of the barkeeps.

Unruffled, Doc tossed off his drink, put the glass on the bar and, colder than hell on the stoker's day off, stepped through the stunned crowd, plainly aiming for the batwings.

Wilson's deputies closed in on him. 'No funny business, Doc.'

'What's the charge?'

'We'll think of something,' Cotton Wilson said nastily.

After the batwings had flapped behind Doc and his coterie of badges the saloon seemed to pick up a new lease on life. A crowd gathered wordlessly about Bailey's body.

Shanssey came into it with uncaring elbows. 'All right. Break it up.' He beckoned over a couple of his girls. 'Get a sheet or one of them table covers; a thing like that can put a cramp in business. You—' he growled, putting the finger on another frail, 'tell them fiddlers to hit up a hornpipe.' He took stock of the crowd that was beginning to pinch off in knots with their heads together. 'Step up to the bar, folks! Drinks on the house!'

While Shanssey was still trying to get his customers back to normal Wyatt drifted into his orbit and carried him down to the far end of the bar. 'It's always a mess after something like that,' the ex-pugilist growled.

'There's one thing you got to say for Doc,' Wyatt said. 'He was plumb at the front when they was passin' out guts.'

'Shanssey! Mr. Earp!' Kate cried, hurrying toward them. 'They hadn't no business taking Doc up for that. You saw what happened! What else could he have done? It was him or Bailey—'

'Now, now,' Shanssey said, harried eyes flicking about, 'Cotton knows—'

Wyatt's hand fell on his arm. 'Who's this?'

35

'Huh? Oh—Kate Fisher. Friend of Doc's. Kate, meet Wyatt Earp—'

'They're going to frame him!' Kate cut in. There was fright in her eyes, in the jump of her voice. She was twisting her chubby jeweled hands together. Her face looked blotchy in the lamp's yellow gleam. 'Do something, can't you? Don't just stand there! This whole pack saw Bailey pull that gun on him—'

'Why don't you just relax,' Wyatt said. 'The law will take care of everything.'

Kate was not to be put off or consoled. She whirled on the detective furiously. 'You fool! There ain't no law on the Flat!'

'Well, it's no business of mine,' Wyatt said, shaking free of her. 'But I'll say this, lady: I never saw a man more determined to get chopped down. And I'll tell you this! I don't like Holliday. I don't want any part of him.'

Kate peered at Wyatt more intently. 'Please, Mr. Earp—'

'Sorry,' Earp said gruffly. 'Good night.'

He turned with a stiff-necked bow and went out.

Kate turned desperately to Shanssey. The saloonkeeper tiredly shook his head. 'I can see that a pair of fast horses are put around at the back of the hotel—that's about as far as I'll be able to go. I wouldn't stay in business ten minutes if it was ever to get out I helped him. A man's got to look at the facts of this matter.'

'Then he's finished,' Kate said; looking

stonily at him. 'He hasn't another friend in this town.'

Shanssey's glance drifted over the grumbling crowd. He saw anger there, and a bleaker note was creeping up through the talk. Kate's knuckles shone white. There was a look in her face he wasn't able to meet.

*   *   *

In the lobby of the Hotel Astor, Earp stood against the counter talking to the desk clerk.

'Be sure you get this telegram off first thing in the morning.'

The clerk nodded as Wyatt signed his name and pushed the pad of yellow paper toward his hand. Cotton Wilson, just then coming down the stairs, spotted Wyatt and froze. But only for a moment. Anger tightened his cheeks and a wave of color crawled up his neck as, with glance averted, he came off the stairs and, stomping across the lobby, went out.

'What's he doing here?' Wyatt said.

'They're holding Holliday upstairs in his room.'

'In his room?' Wyatt's focus widened. Looking puzzled he rasped a hand across his jaw. Twisting around he stared at the street into which the marshal had stepped. Then, chousing his glance toward the stairs, grunting unintelligibly, he started up them.

As he came onto the second landing he saw

the deputy Wayne with his shoulders settled against a closed door. Wyatt went on to his own door, shoved it open with his hand near his pistol and, when nothing untoward happened, went in and cuffed it shut. He stood there beside the bed, grimly thinking. The whole business *did* have a kind of smell.

He finally shrugged and sat down and pulled off his boots. Going over to the dresser he turned down the gas lamp and presently pulled off his shield-fronted shirt. He was hunched there staring at the things in his head when a quick knock rattled the door. Kate Fisher, not waiting for his permission, came in, shutting the door behind her.

She was panting a little from the climb, the agitation of her more obvious charms a bit overpowering seen thus at close quarters stacked against the closed door. She gave him a tight and practiced smile and, when he didn't respond, she caused her bosom to heave agitatedly. Her low-cut gown only emphasized the flesh pushed deliberately by her corsets against the confining cloth. She seemed about to burst from the dress but Wyatt stayed where he was through the gamut of her swift-changing tactics. Now, face twisted, the panic showing, she rushed to the window, ran up the blind and stared into the night-shrouded street below.

'Look,' Wyatt said. 'Like I told you, Miss Fisher, this is none of my business.'

'Think what you will, but that's a lynch mob out there. You've got to do something! Wilson won't lift a finger and they're—listen to them! You hear that?' She was almost beside herself, shaking all over, her eyes like great coals in the pallor of her cheeks. 'They're goin' to hang him, mister! The rights of it don't matter; he's a human bein' ain't he? You goin' to sit there and let them take him out an' string him up?'

Wyatt pulled on his shirt, and got up and shoved the tails in. He went over to the window. He could hear them all right. They were heading for the jail. Kate snarled, 'A pack of goddamn animals!'

He met the full force of her desperation. 'No matter what he done he don't deserve that,' she said hoarsely, grabbing hold of his arm like a bear trap.

Her scent swirled around him in a musky fog. He extricated himself and stepped back. 'I'll do anything,' Kate said. 'Anything you say—'

'Not necessary, ma'am.' Wyatt sat down and pulled his boots on. 'First place, Doc ain't over in that jail, he's right here under this roof.'

He studied her a moment. 'Get down to the end of the street there someplace and watch this window. When I wave a lamp set fire to whatever comes handiest.' Getting a bandanna out of his pocket he tied it over his nose and mouth, jammed on his hat and lifted the gun from his holster. Suddenly she came hard

39

against him with the staves of her corsets, the bulge of her breasts. 'Bless you!' she cried above the noises from the street.

Wyatt pulled open the door. He moved down the hall with a cat-quick stealth, stopping a moment where it turned, his mouth squeezed tight. If this thing backfired there'd be hell to pay. When Earp rounded the corner the big deputy, Wayne, was still lounging against Doc's door. Pistol leveled, Wyatt leaped.

The man, caught cold, stood gaping, frozen. His eyes bulged as though he couldn't believe what they told him. Too late he grabbed left-handed for the doorknob, his right streaking hipward. The barrel of Wyatt's upswinging pistol took him sharply under the jaw. The man went limp and slid down the jamb like a busted sack. Wyatt kicked the door open.

Doc, in a chair by the window, was moodily eyeing the activity below. A startled deputy on the bed blinked incredulously into Wyatt's gun snout. 'Git your paws up!' Wyatt growled.

The deputy let go of his shotgun. Wyatt, stepping in, rapped the pistol against his head. The man folded. Doc's watching face displayed hardly any interest. Smiling thinly he said, 'Guess you're what might facetiously be called an "advance scout" for the necktie—'

'Choke off the blat,' Wyatt said, 'and get out of here!'

'You don't really think I'd be fool enough,

do you? Hells fire! The minute I got off this chair you'd turn that gun on me and claim I tried to duck out on you.'

'We got no time to play games. Get movin'!' Wyatt snapped.

He had dragged Wayne into the room and was binding and gagging the pair methodically. He picked up one of Wayne's pistols and flipped it to Doc, at the same time divesting his face of its mask.

The gambler, now staring, looked genuinely surprised. 'A little out of your line, ain't it, busting loose prisoners?'

'Nothing personal about this,' Wyatt said impatiently. 'I just don't hold with lynchings.' He lifted the lamp from the dresser, went over to the window and waggled it back and forth.

*   *   *

At the far end of Main Street there was an abandoned barn that had once been part of a horse change station. Kate, dressed like a man, saw the flare of light in the hotel window. She took a lighted kerosene lamp off a manger and pitched it into a great pile of musty hay. Flames shot up. She watched them spread, then ducked out the side door.

Back in Doc's room both men stood calmly. Out in the street a loud voice yelled, 'Are you with me?'

A chorus of angry growls rose in answer.

'Somebody git a rope!'

Doc grinned at Earp. 'I'd say that right here and now would be a pretty good time to get out of here if this deal's really on the level.'

'We'll wait a bit.'

'It's your show.' Doc shrugged.

Wyatt, pointing through the window, brought Doc's head around. He saw the leap of red-flecked flames and softly whistled. 'Mighty handy bonfire.'

'Go down the back way.' A discovery shout went up from the street. 'They've seen the fire. Wouldn't lean too hard on my luck if I was you.'

'I'm obliged to you, Tinbadge.' The gambler lifted a hand. 'Look me up some time in Dodge City and I'll try to render a more proper thanks.'

'You can thank me properly by staying out of Dodge.'

Doc, chuckling, stepped into the hall and disappeared. Wyatt took another thoughtful look from the window. The ruse was pulling the mob down the street. Men with buckets were hustling to join them.

Down behind the hotel Doc found Kate with two saddled horses waiting. On the front porch of his establishment John Shanssey smiled and puffed on his cigar as towering flames lit up the back of town.

PART TWO
DODGE CITY

CHAPTER FOUR

A rattling coach behind six horses beat up the dust of the pot-holed road, flinging it over the borders of rabbit brush and thousands of thirsty wild sunflowers. Dead ahead loomed a hill thatched in a haphazard fashion with slabs of weathered wood and a scattering of drunken crosses. A sign, bullet-riddled, read:

BOOT HILL CEMETERY, DODGE CITY.

Some distance along the far side of this hill, not in sight at the moment to driver or passengers, was a yellow-painted depot and the sidings of a railroad. A man with a sweeping well-cared-for mustache stepped out of the depot carrying a packet of letters. For perhaps forty feet he strode along beside the tracks; then, shaking loose of his obvious preoccupation, he crossed the rails and bent his lengthening stride toward the main part of town. He passed a sign, hesitated, turned and stared back at it. He considered it perhaps a bit longer than necessary. There was nothing subtle or elusive about the proclamation. It said bluntly: DEADLINE. CHECK ALL FIREARMS AT MARSHAL'S OFFICE. BY ORDER OF DODGE CITY COUNCIL.

He moved on into the traffic, a tall man

with springy stride yet with the saddlebound carriage of a man more at home on the back of a horse. His eyes were sharp and cold as he scanned passing faces. A number of people spoke to him. He touched his hat to the women and managed a nod for the men, but he did not pause or become engaged in conversation. Straight ahead of him now was the Long Branch Saloon. Across the road from the Marshal's Office was the Dodge House, a smart looking and eminently presentable hotel.

The man paused to stare a moment in the direction of the saloon, then shook off the thought and cut toward the Marshal's Office and the barred windows of the jail. As he came up to the door, Charlie Bassett stepped out.

'By grab, I'm glad to see you, Wyatt!' Bassett was Earp's chief deputy and a very well known marshal in his own right. He said, 'Bat Masterson's in there waitin' to see you.'

Wyatt nodded, got his watch out and checked it. 'Stage is due. Take a squint at the passengers.'

Bassett took off across the street as Wyatt moved into the office.

He found Masterson sitting behind the desk with his boots propped on it and a stump of cigar sticking out of his mouth. Wyatt slapped Bat's feet off the desk, shoved the chair away. Putting one hip on the desk, he placed the letters beside him and opened the top one.

The stagecoach pulled up in front of the Dodge House and commenced unloading, as could plainly be seen through the plate glass of the window.

Masterson lit the ragged end of his cigar and puffed in silence. Wyatt, busily reading, said, 'Letter from Virgil.'

'Understand things are really humming in Tombstone what with that silver strike and the bunch any boom will always draw in its wake. How's Virg doing?'

'Hey!' Wyatt exclaimed. 'He's bought himself a house! Makes the first of us Earps to really put down roots. He says Betty is expectin' again this summer.'

Dropping the top page, Wyatt's face as he continued reading, began to take on the granite set of annoyance. 'Thought so!'

'Bad news?'

Finishing the letter Wyatt tossed it on the desk. 'I was right about those two. Virg tells me Ike Clanton and Ringo rode in a couple weeks ago. Virgil arrested them, but you know how that goes. Ike's old man owns that county. The judge, who's square in the old bastard's pocket, turned 'em both loose. Freed 'em of all charges. Damn! Those lousy killers—turned them scot stinkin' free!'

Tipping back his derby, Masterson rubbed some of the sweat off his forehead. 'Guess I'll never get used to risking my neck pullin' in these hardcases an' watching some tinhorn

47

judge set 'em free.'

'He says Ringo's headin' back up this way.'

'So? What about Ike? He's the one I'd like to get *my* hands on.'

'Virg says Old Man Clanton got killed in an ambush. Ike's staying on to take over the ranch.' Wyatt slammed a fist on the desk. 'I tell you, Bat, I just don't understand it.'

'No thanks in this business—you ought to know that.'

Wyatt shook his head. 'You know, I'm just the town marshal here. But some of the things I've seen and had to put up with . . . You're the sheriff, Bat, so you see more even than I do. How many of these peckernecks have tried to make you a deal?'

'Oh,' Masterson said with a chubby grin, 'I get propositions worth about a thousand bucks a month.'

'Doesn't it bother you?'

The county sheriff shrugged.

'I sometimes wonder,' Wyatt said with a scowl, 'if we wouldn't be exhibiting considerable more sense to take their—'

'Now you know mighty well you couldn't do that.'

'I've sure been givin' it some thought,' Wyatt growled. 'We ain't getting no younger. Be kind of nice to have a stake tucked away—'

The pair of them simultaneously came to their feet and were drawn to the plate glass to stare across the street. A 'classy number,' as

Bat himself put it, had just gotten off the stage and now was standing beside it, graceful as a willow, pointing out her luggage to an attentive half dozen of the town's derby-hatted sports.

Wyatt exclaimed in a gusty breath, 'Talk about your children in the fiery furnace! God above, Bat, who's that?'

'Looks to me like Delilah,' Masterson said, fingering his tie. He ran a considering hand across his cheeks, unconsciously smirking. 'Or Salome—wasn't she the dame that asked for that preacher's head on a platter?' He continued to watch the newcomer admiringly as, trailed by her escort of smitten swains, she moved into the shade of the coach's lean shadow, exchanging a few words with the driver before striking out with her retinue of baggage carriers straight up the street in the direction of Miss Deed's boarding house. 'What do you suppose she's doing in a place like Dodge?'

He got no change out of Wyatt. The Dodge City marshal was staring after her raptly. Bat said, 'Watch out for the flies. You got your hatch dropped open like a hungry bird's.'

Wyatt, flushing, pulled up his jaw.

'That's strictly big city fluff,' Sheriff Masterson said.

'School teacher?' Wyatt guessed.

'Too fancy a getup.'

'Lady rancher, maybe?'

'Too soft, too frilly.' Bat shook his head as the young woman moved out of their sight leaving a myriad of turned heads peering after her. Some cowhand whistled. Several laughing loafers dug each other with their elbows. All up and down the street were visible unmistakable signs of male reaction. Wyatt said reflectively, 'Must be fixin' to stay a while. Two trunks would hold more than a overnight change.'

'Yeah,' Bat said scowling. 'And I've got to take out a posse, fact is, that's what I come to see you about. That daddratted Injun's on the warpath again.'

'Dull Knife?'

Masterson nodded. 'I'm going to have to borry your deputies, chum.'

'Damned if you ain't always shortest of men at the most inopportune times,' Wyatt growled.

Charlie Bassett came in.

'Who's the frail?' Wyatt and Bat popped the question almost in the same breath.

'What frail?' Bassett said, and both the other men groaned.

'Hell, I been too busy to be lookin' out fer wimmen,' Wyatt's chief deputy grumbled. 'Hold your drawers now—I got some real news. Doctor an' Mrs. John Holliday just checked in an' have put up at the Dodge House!'

Both officers blinked. Wyatt said, '*Mrs*. John

Holliday—I didn't know he was married!' And in the next breath he growled, 'I told that damn fool to stay out of Dodge!'

Masterson caught Bassett's arm. 'Lottie Deno? A redhead?'

'Big Nose Kate,' Bassett said, enjoying their concerned surprise.

Wyatt scowled. 'I better get over there before he unpacks—'

'Wait a minute,' Bat grumbled. 'You going to loan me your deputies?'

'All right—all right,' Wyatt gave in, plainly distracted. 'I'll have to keep Charlie, though; he's needed right here. You can have the rest but you better be back before those trail herds pull in. You know what it's like when those cowhands hit town.'

Wyatt paused at the door as though of two minds about something. Coming back he pulled his shell belt from a peg and strapped it about his lean-hipped middle.

He found the consumptive dentist-turned-gambler in the barber shop with his feet up and the towel and apron covering him, stretched out flat in the chair. The barber removed the steaming towel from Holliday's face and painted it with a froth of lather. The gambler spotted Wyatt at once but made out not to notice him. The famous boots were unpolished, the thinning soles were about to show holes, and both heels were run over. For a celebrity, Wyatt thought, Doc looked downright seedy.

'Mario,' Wyatt said, 'go out and get some fresh air.'

'Si, signor.' The barber hurriedly vanished. Wyatt locked the door. Doc, pumping the chair, raised himself to a sitting position and with the apron smeared some of the lather off. 'Ah,' he said caustically, 'I see the mayor hasn't forgotten me.'

'I thought I told you to stay out of Dodge City.' Wyatt wasn't one to beat around any bushes.

Doc, climbing out of the chair, picked up Mario's razor. He ran it back and forth a few times over the strop and tested its edge with the ball of his thumb. 'I like a sharp razor. You come in for a shave?'

'No, thanks,' Wyatt said. 'And this ain't no time for jokes.'

Brushing fresh lather onto his face Doc stepped over to the mirror and started shaving himself.

'A stage,' Wyatt said, 'leaves for Abilene in the morning. You be on it.'

'Can't. Marshal of Abilene sent me here. Matter of fact, I wish some enterprising chap would draft a new speech for tinbadges. In the last five burgs there hasn't hardly been a changed word even.'

'Then you'll hole up in your room until day after tomorrow. I will personally escort you to the westbound train.'

52

'It seems we are faced with a hard fact, Wyatt. You find me in a state of complete financial collapse. I don't even have the price of a ticket.'

'There's still Kate's jewelry. You can fall back—'

'Alas,' Doc said, 'those rocks are but a fond memory. I've had a terrible streak of luck.'

'You had a roll in Fort Griffin thick enough to choke a cow.'

'As you may recall,' Doc smiled, 'I shook the dust of that town in something of a hurry. I went off and left twenty thousand in your friend Shanssey's safe.'

Twisting his head he regarded the marshal sadly.

Wyatt, hunkered now on the arm of the mechanical chair with his gun hand propped upon the grip of his pistol, returned the stare without noticeable feeling.

'And do you know,' Doc sighed, 'what that sonofabitch did? Those two broncs he staked out in back of the hotel cost me exactly ten thousand simoleons apiece! Fancy!' With a philosophical shrug he went back to his shaving. 'Everyone,' he said presently, 'seems to put a most outlandish value on my life.'

Done with his shaving he stepped over to the water bowl and dipped his face into his hands. Groping blindly, he gasped, 'Don't just sit there like a fly in molasses. Pass me that towel before I run into something.'

53

'You're going to run into something if you don't haul your freight out of here.' Wyatt flipped him the towel, watched the man wipe his face off. Now Doc stepped along the shelf, inspecting the labels of the displayed stock of bottles, sniffing with a variety of facial contortions. He uncapped a lavender bottle and helped himself to a swig. 'Not bad,' he said, smacking his lips, and put some on his hair.

'Wyatt,' he said finally, wheeling around to face him squarely, 'how much do you make in a year handling trouble? About a hundred a month and two bucks an arrest? If you were the sort to stash some by on the side you could make quite a bundle. I don't suppose you are, so I'd imagine most of the time the cupboard goes bare.'

'Come to the point if you've got one.'

'I feel compelled,' Doc said delicately, 'to offer you a proposition. How much money can you lay hands on?'

Wyatt considered him, cold faced, in silence.

Doc was not moved to blush. 'Not much, I gather. A few hundreds you've been saving for a ranch or country store? Look,' he said, getting down to bedrock, 'I can make it easy for you to own a *big* spread. I mean something in the neighborhood of a couple thousand head. Stake me for a start and I'll split my winnings with you. When the trail drives hit this burg there'll be real money for a man with

54

his eyes open.'

'Of all the trashy gall—'

'Tish tash,' Doc grinned. 'Don't be so goddam holy! Any number of gents would be delighted to back me for even as little as five percent. You consider yourself better than the mayor of this town? Damn it, I like you, feller. I like your cut.'

'You're a generous bastard,' Wyatt said, getting up.

Doc picked up the folded razor, tossing it up from one hand to the other. 'Look at it this way: What would a barber be without his razor? A boat without a rudder? A church without a steeple? You're a peace officer; how far would you get without a gun? About as far as a carpenter without saw or hammer. My tool is money—coin of the realm.' He considered Wyatt whimsically. 'Don't be a goddam piker. Put up your widow's mite. It'll be in good hands, believe me.'

'You guaranteein' not to lose?'

It was hard to tell if Wyatt were stringing him along or actually thinking of taking Doc up on it.

'You got a good poker face,' Doc sighed. Suddenly he twisted over, taking time out to cough. When the paroxysm passed he wiped his mouth with a white square of linen, studying it a moment before he put it away. 'I never lose when the moon is right. Poker is the game of desperate fools lured on by hope and the need of hard cash. The man who has nothing to lose rakes the pots in. And that's the way I go into a game. It's the game—'

'It's a cinch,' Wyatt scowled, 'you don't care about your hide.'

'With this cough?' Doc laughed bitterly. 'I certainly don't intend to wind up in white sheets! Come on—what are you scared of?'

They stared at each other like a couple of strange dogs.

Doc said with a snort, 'Well, it figures. Dig into that hoard, you damn Simon Legree. If you want me out of here you'll have to pay the train fare.' He said with a contemptuous slanch of the eyes, 'Maybe your precious City Council can be talked into making it up to you!'

Wyatt laughed. 'I've done some pretty stupid things. I think I'm about to do another one and let you stick around.'

Doc cried, 'My God! Such generosity!'

'Guess it's a kind of damn fool admiration for a sport who don't know when to yell calf rope. You can stay,' he said sobering, 'and you can play—on one condition. No knives. No guns. No killin's.'

Doc bowed formally. 'You have my word—as a gentleman.'

'One thing more,' Wyatt said. 'You ought to treat that woman decent or leave her.'

'You mean Kate? She's a cross, no getting around it. Stands for every last thing I hate in

56

myself. I don't know . . .' He sighed. 'I'll try, Wyatt. Leave me two bits for the face-scraper, will you?'

*   *   *

In his office Wyatt, tipped back in his chair, was filing down the firing pin of his new Buntline Special, a pair of which had been presented to him by the author of that horrendous thriller *Buffalo Bill: King of the Border Men* which, in the marshal's candid opinion, was a heap of sure-enough garbage. But the gun, as he twirled it and sat clicking the trigger, he admired pretty highly.

'Hey,' Bassett said, stepping in off the street, 'where'd you get the new pistol? By the way,' he went on, without waiting for an answer (which is the way with a lot of folks even now), 'I found out all about your elegant obsession.'

'My what?' Earp said, peering around the barrel.

'That dame that got off the stage a while ago. Some gun!'

'That's the one that feller Buntline had made up for me special. What about her?'

'Sure beautiful,' Bassett grinned. 'But ain't that barrel too long?'

'You talkin' about this gun or the girl?'

'Hand-tooled, too,' Basset said, sounding envious. 'Some cannon.'

57

'What'd you find out?' Wyatt laid the gun on his desk.

'Why, she's stayin' over there at Miz Deed's place. Along with them drummers. Some of the most elegant foofaraw you ever seen come outa them trunks, they tell me. Some of them things come clean from Paris—that's in France, by godfries! Five foot four, weighs a hundred an' twenty pounds—'

'What's her line?'

'Gambler.'

'Very funny, Charlie.'

'Well, I thought so muself, but it's the Gawd's own truth. Hell, don't take my word for it. Take a hike down to the Long Branch an' see fer yourself.'

Wyatt jumped up and stomped out, Basset trailing him.

*   *   *

A plush joint, the Long Branch, whole notches above the average of its kind. And there, sure enough, sat the girl at the faro bank, bucking the house man, Cockeyed Frank Loving, who was nobody's fool even though he did favor ladies' garters for keeping his sleeves from dropping down over his fingers. A cowhand, half plastered, was also in the play and very evidently endeavoring to impress the girl with his manly charm. At least a dozen men were gathered about the table, including Mayor

Kelly, the owner of record. His triple chins were dripping sweat like a Kansas City hydrant. Wyatt, still trailed by Charlie Bassett, came up and stopped behind the outsize pants Kelly had to buy to cover his bottom. Neither Wyatt nor his deputy was armed.

Kelly looked around. 'What's the trouble, Marshal?'

Wyatt, indicating the girl, said, 'I'm going to bust up the game.'

'Now, wait a minute,' Kelly said, plainly riled. 'You can't come in here and stop my game just because a woman's got her money on the table.'

'Every time we get a woman in a place like this there's a fight. My job's to keep the peace. Close her out.'

When the fat mayor made no move to comply, Earp stepped forward, grabbed the girl's cards and flung them over his shoulder. 'Game's closed.'

The cowhand got to his feet. It appeared to be considerable of an effort, but there was no mistaking the jut of his jaw. 'That's no way to do to a lady!'

'You shut your mouth an' stay out of this, feller.'

The young lady smiled. 'It appears the marshal is laboring under the mistaken idea that he's not dealing with a lady.'

'No *lady* plays cards in a gents' saloon. Not in my book, anyway,' Wyatt said.

'No *gent*,' the cowboy growled, 'would talk like that to a lady.'

The marshal's hard stare made the fellow back up a step. Turning to Kelly, Wyatt said, 'If you'll think back, Mr. Mayor, you'll recollect we both agreed there'd be no women gamblers on the north side of the street.'

'But, Wyatt,' Kelly cried, 'this here is Laura Denbow. Miss Denbow's marker is good for ten grand anyplace in the West. She's considered an exception—'

'Not in Dodge City, she ain't.'

'Come, man—be reasonable!'

'So you're the famous Wyatt Earp,' Laura said. With a flash of dark eyes she added, 'Lawman, judge and jury.'

'That's right,' Wyatt grinned. 'Start with you an' we'll have every tramp on the south side over here.'

'Who's a tramp?' the cowhand bristled.

'Keep out of this, buster.'

Laura stood up and Wyatt nodded toward the door. 'On your way.'

'Is this an arrest?'

'If you mean are you going to jail, the answer's yes.'

Her chin came up. 'On what charge?'

'Expect I'll likely think up a better one. In case I don't, we'll book you for disturbing the public peace.'

She smiled at him, angered. 'Don't you think you'd better wait for a few of your

60

deputy marshals?'

'I think I can manage,' Wyatt said, taking her arm.

The cowboy shoved forward. 'Git your paw offa her!'

He yanked open his jacket, palming a concealed pistol. The crowd backed off with an audible gasp, leaving a good fifteen feet of silence open all around them. Wyatt eyed the man carefully.

The fellow was enjoying the sensation he was creating. He fell into a crouch. 'Go for your gun!'

'Happens I'm not heeled.'

The fellow stared stupidly as the marshal, outwardly cool as the proverbial well chain, moved a couple of steps nearer. The drunk flung up his pistol. 'Stand where you are!' It seemed as though he would surely fire if the badge packer wiggled so much as a finger.

The marshal was used to handling drunks. 'I can see you don't know what you're doing, feller. Better give me that pistol before it gets you into real trouble.'

Bleary-eyed, weaving around on his feet like a rudderless ship in the grip of a tempest, the big slob eared back the hammer of his gun.

Wyatt said with a sneer, 'You haven't got the nerve to pull that trigger.' The cowboy commenced again to back away. 'Stand still!' Wyatt said. 'I'm goin' to take that peashooter away from you.'

Every face around them reflected the tension of not knowing what that damned fool would do. The girl had a hand tight against her lips. The mayor's eyes looked bigger than slop buckets. Sweat beaded the house man's upper lip and Bassett's face was rock stiff with repression as he stood locked in his tracks.

Wyatt bored in, holding the man with his bitter stare. The fellow couldn't back away any farther, the blades of his shoulders were hard against the wall. Sweat ran off his chin, the pistol waggled in his fist, the roll of his eyes showed fright and fury and then, in desperation, he fired into the floor at Wyatt's feet. Wyatt came steadily on until the brims of their hats weren't a foot apart. The fellow, snarling, rammed his gun into Wyatt's belly. Wyatt's hand came up and took the pistol away from him. The man's drunken curse cut the quiet like a sob. Everybody started to talk at once.

The cowboy's voice, crammed with earnestness, whined, 'I didn't aim fer to shoot you, mister. It was jest—'

'Sure, feller. I understand. You just wanted to impress the little lady.'

The whole place, it seemed, heaved a sign of relief. Bassett stepped up. Laura said to Kelly, '*He*'s a showoff, too.'

The fat mayor shook his head, mopping his face. 'Not him!' he exclaimed. 'I've seen him do that too many times. He can read a man's mind like he owned him.'

'Charlie,' Wyatt said, 'take him in the back room and sober him up. Then get him out of town.' Wheeling, taking hold of Laura's arm, he started her toward the door. Kelly, intercepting him, said, 'You're not really serious about this, are you? About arresting Miss Denbow?'

'Out of the way, Kelly. I've had enough for one evenin'.'

'That's all right, Mr. Kelly,' the girl smiled. It took some of the strain cut of her cheeks, but her tone made it plain she considered the marshal two shades lower than the belly of a snake. 'I intend to know every cranny of this town, and I might just as well start in with the dungeons.'

She pulled her arm away, brushed his touch from her sleeve and walked, head erect, ahead of him to the louvered doors. There she stopped and stepped aside.

Wyatt looked at her, puzzled.

'Aren't you going to open them for me?'

Wyatt's cheeks turned red, his eyes flashed with annoyance. Then he shoved the doors open and followed her out, leaving Kelly and the others staring after them open-mouthed.

CHAPTER FIVE

The girl got under Wyatt's skin as no other woman had been able to do. She was different, a type he had never before come up against though he'd met many kinds. Her cool, aloof self-sufficiency rubbed sparks from his temper, and the more he tried to figure her out the greater was his hotly baffled confusion. She was a beauty—he gave her that—and she had courage, but it was a kind of courage bluntly bordering on boldness he couldn't understand. If she *was* a lady—and she sure as hell looked it—why was she determined to spend her time in saloons?

The jail back of his office held a long line of cells, and he steered her to one near the farther end. Directly across from the one he had in mind was the nauseating sight of a beat-up and passed-out drunk loudly snoring. Laura, taking in these unpleasant surroundings, visibly stiffened and faced him indignantly. 'Do you have to put me here?'

'You could get ten days for this, and ought to. I treat everyone alike. No preferential treatment regardless of sex,' Wyatt said, remembering the opinion of him she had so freely expressed to the mayor.

'But all I've done—'

'You can tell it to the judge.'

64

'Are you always so obnoxious?'

'Don't push me, ma'am. I can git a lot more so.'

She was riled, all right. Her chin came up. She looked about as put out as he felt. 'Very well. Do your damndest.'

Wyatt grinned. 'You can leave right now if you want to give me your promise to do all your gambling south of the line.'

She had herself in hand now. She said, smiling sweetly, 'I wouldn't want you to break any rules for my benefit.' She stepped into the cell, nostrils quivering daintily. 'Go ahead, lock me in. We can't have you being remiss in your duty.'

Wyatt glared. Seething, wild with frustration, he grabbed the grille and slammed it shut.

'My, what a temper! Well, perhaps the judge, at least, if he isn't more impartial may not be so sternly righteous. Hell hath no fury like a righteous man.' She was laughing at him openly, enjoying his indignant confusion. 'Here,' she said, reaching through the bars to push into his hands a number of Long Branch chips she'd come off with. 'I won't need these here. Go out and buy yourself a new halo.'

Wyatt gnashed his teeth, wishing he had a dog to kick. Then, reluctantly, a sort of parched grin cracked his lips as he studied the straight slim line of her back. He was a man who could not pass up a challenge, and the sparks this girl had so easily struck from him stung like nettles in his mind, stirring unaccustomed thoughts and sleeping desires he had figured to be done with.

*   *   *

Night again shook out its sable blanket and the lights of Dodge gleamed over the prairie like a swirl of thrown brilliants. Doc, lugging a bottle, came into the Marshal's office, steadily enough but in an aura of fumes that threatened to lift the paint right off the walls.

Charlie Basset, elbow deep in paperwork, threw down his chewed pencil and pushed back with a groan. 'Man, this twelve on twelve off is playin' hell with my home life. These goddam papers would rub the ass off an elephant. What's stickin' you?'

Doc, hauling up a chair, brushed the papers aside and set down his bottle and an unopened deck of cards. 'Have a nip?'

'I wouldn't mind, by Gawd,' Bassett said, 'but I reckon not. Wyatt won't stand for drinkin' on duty. What's the occasion?'

Doc poured a slug down his throat and corked the bottle. He broke open the cards and laid out a deal of blackjack. 'Well,' he said, examining his hand, 'I'd like to bail out that woman.'

'Denbow?'

'That her name? Never seen a piece that

66

looked any better put together.'

Bassett squinted at his cards. 'Hit me, damn it. I've got nineteen.'

'Twenty,' Doc said, and dealt again. 'How about it?'

'She's got to appear in court tomorrer. No bail's been set. I'll stand on these.'

Doc hit himself three times hand-running. 'Twenty-one. I'll wait for Wyatt.'

Bassett vigorously scratched his head. He watched Doc toss around the pasteboards. 'I sure hope Masterson gits back with our deppities before them goddam cowboys hit town. Blackjack!'

'I've got one, too.'

'You musta fell in the manure pile.' Bassett glared. 'Nothin' personal, Doc, but you know, if we was playin' fer real, I'd be compelled, by Gawd, to hev a look at that deck.'

'An' I'd be forced, was that the case, to see you try and get it,' Doc confided imperturbably.

Charlie Bassett made a playful pass at his pistol. Doc's lightning reflexes took hold at once. Before Bassett's gun was half out of its holster, Doc's pistol was looking him square in the face. Bassett gaped and Doc grinned. 'You could get yourself killed trying that sometime.'

'Hell, you didn't think I was sure-enough tryin', didja?' He peered at Doc slanchways. 'It's almighty lucky Wyatt don't let us go around draggin' our irons or this goddam

67

place would be depopolated!' He scowled around at the clock. He got to his feet. 'Time to check the pris'ners an' lookit the horses. Watch the office, Doc, will yuh?'

'Sure thing, Charlie.'

Bassett tramped through the door to the jail.

Doc sauntered over to the gurrack and lifted down a rifle. He sat down at Wyatt's desk with it cradled on his knees. Presently, still sitting there, he cocked his head to one side and slipped a finger through the trigger guard. A man never knew in a place like Dodge if the sound of a boot heralded friend or foe and the chances, to Doc's practical mind, looked overwhelmingly in favor of it being the latter. He thought it better to be ready and worked the bolt of the weapon. Propping both elbows in the desk top he took dead aim at the door.

Wyatt stepped in.

Doc pulled the trigger.

The unloaded rifle clicked.

'You know,' Doc said, 'I never could get the hang of these things.'

'Move,' Wyatt growled. 'Where's Charlie?'

Doc got up and replaced the rifle. Wyatt, taking Doc's seat, began to leaf through the batch of papers the deputy had been working at.

'He just stepped out for a minute,' Doc said. 'Wyatt, I'd like to bail out Miss Denbow.'

Earp glanced up. 'This personal or otherwise?'

'Otherwise, naturally. Anyone with half an eye could tell she's a sure-quill lady.'

'No favors,' Wyatt said, scowling.

'How about releasing her in exchange for some information?'

'I can't think what you might know that could be of any use to me.'

Doc said, smiling, 'How well do you know Shanghai Pierce?'

'Well enough to stay away from him. Owns about a third of Texas. Used to drive his cattle up the Chisholm to Wichita when I was marshal there a few years back.'

'Expect you've likely had a few run-ins with him?'

'Know of anyone who hasn't? Had to bat him over the cabeza one time when he got tanked up on tarantula juice and tried to shoot up the town. He ain't no creepin' terror—just another damn fool that forgot to grow up.'

'They tell me he's got a real sharp memory.'

'I hurt his pride probably a heap worse'n I did his mule-stubborn head.'

'Well, mister, he's fetching a herd to Dodge City. On his way right now—coming over the Western Trail to save money. I understand when he heard you were packing tin here he vowed to bust this town wide open. Hear he's hired Ringo to make mighty sure you don't spoil his fun. In addition to that, the story is

69

he's put a thousand dollars on your scalp—if it's lifted.'

Wyatt grinned. 'What else is new?'

'That ought to be new enough for most anyone. I find it pretty amusing, putting a price on a lawman's head.'

Wyatt said patiently, 'You know what's the matter with that bunch of wild Indians?'

'I'm always interested in the other man's theory.'

'They're lonely men. That's what's back of all these benders they go on. Those yahoos hit civilization about once a year and by that time they've worked up so damn much steam they've got to do something scandalous or bust their britches. They're just little boys, really, screamin' for attention.'

'They generally get it,' Doc said dryly.

Wyatt nodded. 'We give'em whisky and women and action at the tables, so long as they keep to the south side of the street. But as long as I'm the law around here not one of that bunch crosses the deadline with a gun. Not if it's Shanghai Pierce or Jefferson Davis.'

'Spoke like a gent,' Doc nodded, grinning. 'I'll make sure those words are repeated at your funeral. Now how about turning the little lady loose?'

'She's in good hands right where she is.'

'But, damn it, man, we made a deal!'

'You made the deal. I don't remember agreeing to anything.'

Charlie Bassett came in. 'Charlie,' Doc said, 'you're working for a crook.'

'Go on home and turn in,' Wyatt told him. 'I'll finish up these blasted reports.'

Bassett, stretching, said, 'Obliged. The town's quiet. Night, gents.' Almost through the door, he turned back. 'You really ought to turn that girl loose, boss. She's got no business cooped up behind bars.'

'That's just the way I want it,' Wyatt scowled. 'No business for her means no broken heads.'

Bassett, shrugging, went out.

'I think Charlie's right,' Doc put in.

Wyatt, grinning sourly, flipped a set of keys across the desk. 'I guess I'm gettin' old. Go ahead and let her out.'

'It's your conscience, Earp.'

Wyatt sighed. 'I don't know what it is. Soft spot in my head, I guess likely. That girl's got something.'

'Wouldn't have guessed you'd taken the trouble to notice.'

'I noticed, all right. Tell Kelly she's got to play in the side room. I won't have her gamblin' on the main floor. I mean that. Now clear out of here before I change my mind.'

Doc set off for the cells. Wyatt, taking a deep breath, scowled morosely at the mess of unfinished papers before him. He could hear the mumble of Doc's voice back in the corridor, the tap of high heels and the tramp

71

of Doc's boots that, once again, shone like bottle glass.

The pair came in. Doc tossed the keys on the desk. Wyatt, frowning formidably, made out to be powerfully busy but he heard Laura come up behind him, stand waiting. Grinning in spite of himself he got out of his chair and held open the door for her.

'Thank you, Mr. Earp.'

'You're entirely welcome, Miss Denbow.'

She went out, followed by Doc, who threw an amused glance back across his shoulder at the marshal.

For a while Wyatt just sat there, peering out across the street in the direction in which she had vanished.

CHAPTER SIX

It was early in the morning—almost time for the sun to get up. The interior of the Long Branch, practically deserted, presented a pretty dreary picture and one that stank to high heaven of dead cigars, spilled beer, human sweat and other noxious odors too numerous and well mixed at this hour to be accurately catalogued—even by a connoisseur, of which several haggard-looking specimens were still wandering, ghoul-like, about among the wreckage.

Behind the bar the town's fat mayor and one of the house men, natty dough-faced, quick-fingered Luke Short, were counting up the cash. The main floor with only a couple of lamps still burning looked a rather unpalatable cross between an abandoned parlor house and a mortician's workshop after the corpses have been scrubbed and planted. Only Kate was still standing there pouring it into her.

For the past forty minutes she had been dividing her flushed and venomous attention between the oily roil of what she was drinking and the split curtains off yonder beyond which a poker game was still in grim progress. Killing the bottle she dropped it thumping on the floor and with a do-or-die expression moved belligerently to the curtains which she flung somewhat viciously apart to disclose the heads bent over the table.

First to come under her bitter scrutiny was Doc in his shirtsleeves and black silk tie. There were four other players, including Cockeyed Frank Loving, but Kate's glare lingered longest and most uncharitably on Laura.

Laura said, 'Calling my raise, Doc?'

'Nope—you can have it.' He tossed his hand in.

Laura, grinning, raked in the checks (they were seldom called 'chips' in those days) and teasingly turned over her hand to reveal nothing more ominous than a pair of lone deuces. Doc laughed, gulped some whisky and

73

broke into a cough.

While the cards were going their rounds again, Kate, coming forward, stopped behind Doc's chair. 'Don't you fools know it's damn near morning?'

'Eh?' Loving said.

Doc ignored her, concentrating on his hand.

Kate, cheeks darkening, put a hand on his shoulder. 'For Christ's sake, Doc! You going to sit here all day?'

Doc, shoving a stack of checks into the middle, said, 'I'll open for a hundred.' Reaching into a pocket then he pulled out a bill which he passed over his shoulder without ever lifting his glance from the cards. 'Here—go buy yourself a drink.'

Kate grabbed the banknote and stormed back out to the bar.

The deal went around three or four times more. 'I guess I'll call it a night,' Laura said. 'Frank, cash me in.' She did look tired, for a fact.

All the men stood up as she got out of her chair. Doc put the wrap from the chairback over her shoulders. Wanly smiling her thanks she stowed her winnings in her purse. 'Gentlemen, good night.'

Doc bowed over her hand, quite the gallant.

Laura pushed through the curtains and came up to the bar where she stopped beside Kate.

'Good night,' Laura said softly.

Kate turned her back and, snatching up her glass, drained it.

Laura, turning away, went over and touched up her hair at a mirror and headed for the batwings.

Kelly, peering across Short's shoulder, said, 'Good night, Miss Denbow.'

'Good night, Kelly.'

Wyatt was leaning against a porch post as Laura came out. 'Ah—Miss Denbow?'

She attempted to brush past him but he moved into her path.

'It's late,' she said, 'and I'm pretty well beat, Marshal.'

'Figured to walk you home—'

'I can find the way, thanks.'

Stepping around him, she set off down the echoing scarred planks of the walk. But Wyatt, coming up behind her, caught hold of her shoulders and compelled her to face him.

'Now, look here,' he said gruffly, 'we'd better have an understanding.'

'About what? I've already sampled the hospitality of your jail.'

She had, Wyatt thought, an exceptionally nice voice. It could do things to him, even cool as it was now. 'Well,' he said, trying to make out her face in this rather poor light, 'I think you're onto the fact by now my main obligation around here's to keep the peace. This afternoon, for instance, there could easy have been a killing. I believe I'm entitled to

75

your full cooperation. Going along with this assumption. I'm afraid I've got to insist you keep off the streets at this time of night without you're suitably escorted.'

'I think I've discovered the drift of that thought. You—being so devout, righteous and dedicated—no doubt feel there is no one so eminently suitable to accompany me as yourself. I find this extremely flattering but I prefer to enjoy this fresh air by myself.'

'Look—' Wyatt pleaded, coming as near an apology as he could manage to bring himself. 'I had to do what I did. I'm sorry if you were humiliated. The safety of this whole town was involved. Can't you see that?'

She considered him intently, finally shook her head. 'I'm afraid not. Now, if you will please let me go—'

'Not,' Wyatt said, 'till we call off this war.'

She took a step. She took another, then turned slowly.

'You're truly sorry?'

'Indescribably.'

'Well—I do admire a man who can be big enough to admit he may have been mistaken.' He thought her eyes looked brighter, gayer. 'Do you go that far?'

'I think I could go a heap farther—with you.'

'That was nice.'

He offered his arm. 'May I see you home?'

She hesitated so long he thought she was

76

going to refuse. Then she nodded, smiling, and took hold of his arm. 'I suppose you always get your way?'

'I was never in my life so scared I wasn't going to.'

They both laughed at that and moved off down the walk.

Presently, arriving at an intersection, they paused to consider a dark row of frame houses set behind white picket fences. 'Nice here now,' Laura said. 'It seems so peaceful.'

'It can get pretty rough when the cattle drives hit town.'

'Aren't you ever afraid? You live so dangerous a life.'

'I've been afraid plenty. It's something a man never really gets used to.' They moved on, walking more slowly. 'Laura—I sure ain't hankering to run any chances of damaging this new friendship, but there's something I'm kind of curious about.'

'Nothing ventured, nothing gained.'

'I guess I'm just old-fashioned about women. Call it what you will, but—dang it, you just don't belong in a gambling hall.'

She was silent so long he was certain he had offended her perhaps irretrievably. In a low voice she said, 'Where do I belong?' Then she said, her tone more brittle, 'With the girls south of the line?'

'You know I didn't mean anything like that.'

'I don't suppose you did. I expect you would

like to see me behind a desk teaching school, or running a dry goods store, or perhaps as the wife of some broad-backed horny-handed farmer. Look, Wyatt: If you prefer to go through life as a human target, grant me at least the right to live mine. I don't question your business. Why should you question what I do?'

'Because you're a *woman*,' Wyatt growled.

'And it's a man's world, isn't it? Men have all the fun. Women are expected to stay home and have babies. Women have got to be above reproach—it's all so ridiculous. Why should you think women are greatly different from men? They're not, believe me. They have desires and needs and areas of fulfillment— very often the same dreams and motivations which actuate men. Try to understand that women are human, too. We have our weaknesses, and not always the ones most attributed to us.'

'But can't you see that people will talk?'

'That's one thing you can't stop, marshal or no. Talk is a universal failing—what is it the Scriptures say? "Out of the mouth..." She looked at him steadily. 'Really, Wyatt, you can't change human nature. You just have to live with it like anyone else.'

Wyatt said stubbornly, 'Where are you going? Where have you been?'

'Where I've been is my business; it concerns no one else. As for where I am going—who

78

knows? Who really cares? How many people you know have any real convictions of what they want out of life? Do you understand what *you* want? Perhaps I'll have a house in 'Frisco some day, a white house with green shutters on top of Nob Hill.'

'We all get what we set our sights on.'

'You don't really believe that, do you? Do you honestly imagine the poor enjoy their poverty? Or that the bad enjoy retribution? There are compulsions in people, deep dark places filled with all manner of—'

'Laura,' Wyatt said impatiently, 'what do you want?'

'I want a little time in the sun, my share of fun, adventure, excitement. Do you find that so strange? I can tell you very quickly what I *don't* want. I don't want what my mother and sister had. You'd call it 'homesteading.' I call it legalized slavery.'

'You could marry some big cattle raiser.'

'Why should I? I'm not interested in cattle. It's people that intrigue me.'

'You'll meet some pretty poor types in a gambling hall.'

'Anyone will gamble, given the price and opportunity. Don't be so stuffy. The reason what I'm doing gets under your skin is that I simply refuse to play by the rules a bunch of men have set up to govern a woman's conduct. If you were a woman would you be satisfied with the crumbs?'

'We're not talkin' about me.'

'How like a man,' Laura said, turning her back on him.

'Why try so hard not to be a woman?'

She came around with a soft little laugh. 'Oh, Wyatt,' she exclaimed, 'sometimes you're so veritably a man I could scream. I've seen most of what the West has to offer, from brawls and gunfights to marauding redskins. I don't care what you say about me, or what you think. No man alive is ever going to make me pull a plough for him.'

'That pretty face of yours is sure deceivin'. You've got a heart that's nothing but solid rock.'

'Let's just say,' Laura smiled, 'I don't intend to be bound by old-fashioned ideas about womanhood. Women ought to have the same rights as men. What's sauce for the gander is cream for the goose.'

'At least you play your cards in good style.'

'Why not? I like to gamble. It's my trade. I expect we had better say good night here.'

'Do we have to? I mean, right now?'

'Tomorrow's another day in my business. Good night, Marshal.'

Wyatt stood there, silent, watching the swish of her skirt disappear in the shadows of the lilacs about the porch to Mrs. Deed's boarding house. Even after he heard the soft close of the door he continued to stand there, lost in his thoughts.

*   *   *

The next day in the office, seated back of his desk, Wyatt, his hands smeared and oily, was cleaning a gun when Charlie Bassett came in and tossed a telegram before him.

Unfolding the message Wyatt scanned the lines, frowning. 'From the Attorney General. More trouble, goddam it. Here—see what you make of it.' Wyatt went back to his gun.

Bassett, reading, said, 'Old Ritchie Bell, eh? So him and a couple more halfwits cleaned out a bank at Salina yesterday. Nipped off with some government dough and left a dead teller. Took off down the River trail—'

'An' would I go out and intercept them please!' Wyatt snorted and then sagged back with a sigh. 'Left Salina yesterday. Ought to be somewhere around here tonight, or tomorrow mornin' early. That Bell's a mean actor. I better find someone to go with me. Charlie, you're going to have to hold down the town yourself.'

Wyatt stood up and clapped on his hat.

Bassett grinned. 'Oh, and Jud says he can wangle you an appointment as U. S. Marshal any time you want it.'

'United States Marshal. Yeah, that's all I need.' Wyatt took down a rifle from the rack and went out the door stuffing cartridges in his pockets.

Doc, over at the Long Branch, was whiling away his spare time at the bar, appearing extremely debonair in his usual brushed and black immaculate coat and trousers, ruffled white shirt and black string tie. No one else appeared to be about except Kelly who, in galluses and shirtsleeves, sat at a nearby table looking over his inventory sheets. Wyatt, coming in, stopped by the mayor. 'I got to borrow Luke Short. Ritchie Bell pulled a job in Salina. I just got a wire the bastard's headed this way.'

Kelly shook his head, peering up at Wyatt as though it bothered him real bad to have to be so disappointing. 'Damn—I sent Luke over to Abilene.' He clucked his tongue three or four times against the clack of his dentures. 'How soon you have to pull out?'

'Right away,' Wyatt scowled, 'if I'm going to do any good. Of all the lousy . . . With all my boys bein' away, Luke was the likeliest man still around. It's got to be somebody who can handle a gun. Wire says there's three of them . . .'

'What about Charlie Bassett?'

'Somebody's got to keep an eye on this town.'

Doc, coming down off his stool, caught hold of the marshal's shoulder as Wyatt was about

82

to step into the street. 'I can handle a gun. I'm not busy.'

'You?' Wyatt grunted. 'No, thanks. Some other time maybe.'

'I know which end the smoke comes out of. Of course, if you're looking for testimonials . . . Those best able to give me the nod are regrettably not available.'

Wyatt, not warming to his grin, said, 'I'll handle it.'

Doc, shrugging, turned away. 'Makes me no difference. Go on out and get killed if you want to. I don't guess anyone's going to cry in their beer.'

Wyatt pulled up. He *could* use Doc. To think, with Wyatt, was pretty generally to act. 'It ain't like to do those duds any good, but if you can stand it I can. Raise your right hand. You solemnly swear to uphold the laws . . . Oh, for Pete's sake! This is ridiculous! Consider yourself deputized. Hustle over to my office and get yourself a rifle. I'll go pick up the horses.'

'Hell—don't I get to wear a tin star?'

Wyatt measured him sardonically and laughed. 'Not on your life!'

*   *   *

Once they got onto the road and away from town Wyatt and his unaccustomed deputy put their horses into a lope, regularly alternating

83

between that gait and a walk, making good time, pausing occasionally to let the horses blow. This was rolling country, a lot of it brush covered, ideal for an ambush. 'That Bell,' Doc said, 'is a pretty sorry specimen, tricky as a part-time whore.'

'Man gets all kinds in this business,' Wyatt said. 'Sometimes I wonder why the hell I stay with it.'

They talked in a desultory fashion during the times when they were letting the horses catch up with their wind, but it was mostly small talk, nothing of any importance. Doc was in a philosophical mood; a good many of his remarks were strictly over Wyatt's head and sounded pretty loco. After some while, climbing along hill, Holliday said, 'Don't you reckon it's about time we were getting off this road?'

'We'll have a look from the top, there. Be getting dark before long.'

'You think they're going to stay with the road?'

'Right around here they haven't got much choice. Broken land over to the left there, pretty stony off to the right. Ritchie'll probably be trying to make time, riding with one eye peeled on their back trail. After killing that teller he won't be hunting no posies.'

They, by this time, had gotten pretty well up to the crest. Wyatt put out his hand and got down, Doc somewhat stiffly following suit.

'We'll sneak us a bit of a look,' Wyatt said. 'Main thing is, don't stand out where you can be spotted. Take off that hat. Get a handful of brush you can hold in front of you. We'll have to get down and belly up on it.'

'I'll leave that to you,' Doc said. 'I'll just stand here. This rig set me back too much to screen gravel with.'

Wyatt injuned up to high ground. The sky was ablaze with the sun's dying plunge, all streaky with cobalt and copper. Below him now was a considerable view, fairly level open country. He beckoned Holliday up with the horses.

'You think they've got across those flats already?'

Wyatt shook his head. 'They won't come that way. Probably swung east at the river fork. It's my guess those polecats are heading for Newton.'

'Maybe we'd better get whacking.' Doc, taking another pasear at the country, pointed and said, 'Why wouldn't they come that way?'

'Too apt to be crawling with Indians. I think we'll camp right here for the night. In the morning—'

'You mean we've got to sleep on the *ground*?'

'Hell, that ground ain't so bad. You'll be asleep before you know it.'

'Yeah? And who do you think's going to watch out for my hair?'

85

Wyatt laughed and commenced unsaddling the ponies.

Actually their camp was a little below the rim and on the Dodge City side in the lee of some house-sized boulders. Doc, hunkered as near the tiny fire as he could get, was feeding himself beans with a spoon from a tin plate on his knees. Their only other nourishment was coffee; Doc had forgot to bring along a bottle and was feeling its absence keenly. Wyatt got up and cleaned his plate out with sand. It was full dark now and off to the west somewhere a coyote was yapping like a roomful of women. Saddles and bedrolls were spread close by. After Doc got through with his plate he had a sharp coughing spell that left him gasping. 'Must be this goddam altitude,' he wheezed. 'Sure you didn't fetch along a little nip?'

'Never use it.'

'Sometimes I find it hard to think of you as human.'

Wyatt grinned. 'You'd be better off yourself if—'

'Don't tell me how to run my life.'

'For a smart gambler you sure play sucker odds with that whisky. Keep on and you'll be dead inside a year.'

Doc snorted. 'This kind of a cough doesn't go away.'

'Get out of those stinking saloons and find out. Go live in the mountains. Keep regular hours, get plenty of sleep. You might even live to a ripe old age.'

'Not me. I've seen too many of 'em dodderin' around. When my time comes I figure to go quick. No dragging it out in a bed for me!' He contemplated Wyatt darkly. 'The only thing I'm rightly scared of is dying, by God, in a lousy bed. Never could stand pain. Fair gives me the willies even to think of going little by little like the drip of a faucet. I'm waiting for some sonofabitch to out-shoot me so don't bother preaching me sermons.'

'That why you come along? To get shot?'

'I've been sticking around Dodge hoping to even the account, to find you in some kind of jackpot where the quickness of an eye, a finger on the trigger, could make the difference. I'm giving you the God's unvarnished truth. I've got just one debt in the whole stinking world and I don't like owing it to you.'

Wyatt wasn't sure whether he could believe that or not, but he said in a tone that sounded equally belligerent, 'You don't owe me a thing. I been shiftin' for myself ever since I could button my pants. I never leaned on anyone yet and I don't, by God, figure to lean on you!'

He got up and prepared to turn in, still scowling. From his own pad over in the rocks Doc said, 'I sure would like to depend on that.'

'Far as I'm concerned you can get on that horse an' take off right now.'

Doc grinned nastily. 'I'll stick around a spell. You might crack up yet.'

87

'Don't hold your breath for it.'

'Well,' Doc croaked, 'I give in that you may fool me but the odds are eighty to one that you don't. Tougher they come the harder they fall. A man can only live so long under pressure; something's got to give and when it does you've seen the end of him. Show me a tinbadge, I'll show you—'

'You won't show me nothing!'

Doc, crawling into his blankets, laughed. 'How many lawmen do you know that's old as Wilson? You want to wind up like him? Licking the boots of a bunch of cheap grifters! Never was a star-packer didn't have an Achilles' heel. You ever hear the story of Achilles, Wyatt?'

Wyatt's face in the dim curl of firelight looked taut. His eyes winnowed down, his lips writhed but only a splutter of snarl came forth.

'What's the matter, Preacher?' Doc said with sly malice. 'Aren't you enjoying the sermon? If the boot don't fit kick it off; a man don't have to drink just because somebody shoves a glass at him. You know, honestly now, you and I have got a lot of things in common. We're actually pretty much alike if you want to scratch under the external—'

'Oh, for Christ's sake,' Wyatt cried, 'shut up an' go to sleep.'

*   *   *

He didn't know how long he'd been lying there, blanket up to his chin, staring skyward, trying to count stars and not having too much luck with it. Doc's gurgling snores had choked off in a fit of coughing. The marshal, getting up on an elbow, tried to make out the gambler beyond the fire's feeble shine. The coughing continued. Wyatt, getting out of his blankets, gathered them up and, stepping over the fire, put them down across Doc and went back to his saddle and hunkered there beside a rock, staring drearily into the flaking coals. Though he hated to admit it, Doc's words had stuck with him. What if the sonofabitch was right?

Wyatt shivered in spite of himself. Didn't make no difference how much iron a man had in his nerve he was bound to have some off moments. You only had two eyes and with the deck rigged against you the chances of survival in a place like Dodge ...

The fire, the next time Wyatt jerked his head up to check on it, only showed a few cats-eye embers dully gleaming through the smudge of its ash. Evidently a considerable time had elapsed. Doc lay flat on his back, hat over his face, sounding by God just like old Petey's saw mill that time it had been getting ready to break completely down.

There wasn't any moon. He couldn't make Doc out none too plain, what with all the shadows; he couldn't even manage to doze off again, either. Some sixth sense—call it hunch if you want to—had set off some kind of alarm in Wyatt's head, and the longer he possumed there furtively and, yes by God! *spookily* flirting his eyes around, the stronger this conviction of peril became.

He was too old in the ways of violence to tip his hand by any quick movement or an attempt to alert his companion.

The feeling got ranker, became an alien presence, split up and gradually materialized as three deeper darknesses, creeping nearer, growing plainer, abruptly reared up into the shapes of men with guns drawn.

An arm lifted and pointed out Wyatt's rifle, too far from Wyatt's reach to break any bones in this bastardly bind. While its discoverer bent down to remove it from temptation, the other pair turned their attention on Wyatt.

These were lifting their pistols when out of the blanket-shrouded mound of Doc's raucous snorts and sundry gurgles came three hammering reports and lances of orange flame. At almost this very instant Wyatt's own pistol blasted the night. Three caught-cold shapes toppled grotesquely in their tracks as the marshal sprang up with lifted Colt to make sure certain.

'I thought,' Doc said querulously, 'you were asleep.'

'No,' Wyatt said. 'Not quite asleep.'

'Well, it's done now. Let's head in. I've had enough of communing with nature. Take me a week to get these cricks ironed out of me.'

'What's your hurry? Settle back. They're not goin' anyplace. I've got me some sleep to catch up on.'

Doc peered at him, disgusted. But, finally twisting the riddled blankets around him after carefully making sure he'd whacked out all the sparks, he lay back in smoldering silence.

CHAPTER SEVEN

The following sun-blasted hours looked well into the shank of another hot evening when Wyatt and his consumptive deputy, jogging tired horses down Front Street, pulled up and dismounted in front of Wyatt's office. Charlie Bassett stepped out with a grin. 'Welcome home.' Doc looked just about fit for the scrap heap.

'Guess I'd better fix up the coroner's reports.' Wyatt cuffed the dust from his clothes. 'You're relieved of your obligation, Doc.'

'Not, by God, until the debt's paid in full!'

'It's paid as far as I'm concerned.'

After the marshal went into his office Bassett said, cocking an eyebrow curiously at Doc. 'Get all three of them, did you?'

'I never done so much digging before in my life.'

'Must have been some fancy shooting.'

'Look,' the gambler said irascibly, 'I don't want to hear no more about it.' He surveyed his ruined finery with a scowl. 'You want to do me a favor, go find Kate and tell her to get up to the hotel straightaway. By God, I never felt . . . Just tell her to get over there, will you?'

'Matter of fact,' Bassett said, 'Kate hasn't been around today.'

Doc blinked at him stupidly. 'Hasn't been around?'

'Nobody's seen her on this side since you rode out.'

Doc broke into another coughing spell. He really looked bad, Bassett thought, and moved forward. But Doc brushed him away. 'Send a sawbones up.' He turned and staggered away.

Inside his room, some couple of hours later, Doc sat sprawled rather woozily in an overstuffed chair with the usual bottle and glass propped beside him, a book in one hand, pink-smeared handkerchief in the other. He was coughing again as Kate, without knocking, pushed open the door and stepped inside.

Gravel-voiced, Doc said, 'Where the hell have you been?'

'Out.'

'Where?'

'For a walk.'

'A two-day walk?'

'Well, you've been away, ain't you? Gallivantin' all over with high and mighty Mr.

92

Virtue—'

'I was sick last night. Sick when I came in today. I should think—since I'm paying the ills—you would—'

'Why don't you put a rope around my neck an' jerk on it when you want me?'

Doc rockily picked himself out of the chair. 'You were across that goddamn line, that's where you were!'

'What if I was!'

'Don't get flip with me, you whore! You can't stay away from them, can you? Always got to be gettin' back into your gutter—'

'Way you treat me that's where I belong! What the hell do you care?'

'Who was it this time?'

'Why don't you leave me the hell alone!'

'I think I will,' Doc told her grimly. 'I've had about enough of your whims an' tantrums. You're getting out of here for good. Go on, you slut—go on over there and wallow with the rest of the Good Time Gerties.'

'You ain't ditchin' me,' Kate snarled. 'Not after all I've put up with!'

Doc staggered wobbly-legged over the carpet and reeled through the door that let into Kate's room. He stumbled over to the closet and started throwing out her dresses.

'That damned Wyatt Earp!' Kate screeched. 'He's the one that's turned you against me!'

'You're loco. He's got nothing to do with you. I owe him a debt of honor and I'll pay it, by God, if it kills me!'

'You still playin' the Georgia gentleman? What the hell do you know about honor! You an' your hoity-toity—'

Doc, with a snarl, shoved her sprawling onto the bed. He went back to the closet and yanked down more dresses, whirling to pitch them out into the room.

'Mr. Virtue! Mr. Virtue! Mr. Virtue!' shrieked Kate.

Doc kicked the dresses across the floor to the window, jerked up the sash and pitched the whole tangled mass of them down into the street. He hauled her trunk through the doorway and out onto the stairs. With an angry shove of his brush-scarred boot he sent it crashing below. Then he whirled, grabbed Kate and, dragging her swearing and scratching across the floor, shoved her after it and slammed the door. The balustrade saved her. She came back to stand pounding and screeching like a fishwife.

'Let me in! Let me in!'

Doc, slumped exhausted against the locked door, was doubled over, gasping, face congested . . .

*   *   *

Wyatt, several days later, riding along at a canter over the roll of yellow prairie, turned abruptly off the road and at a walk reined his horse up the rise of a boulder-strewn ridge. Reaching the top, hardly daring to hope, he stood up in his stirrups and peered under the shade of his hand toward a distant arroyo, a shallow gulch off to the left that greenly flanked a dry wash.

She was there. His heart leaped when he saw her standing beside her calico horse beneath the over-hanging branches of a huge cottonwood. Not the lady gambler he knew in town but a different Laura, less austere, more piquantly feminine in boots, split suede skirt and an open-necked blouse of pale blue silk, and with her corn-colored hair braided in pigtails. To Wyatt she looked wholesome and fresh as he sent his horse cantering down the decline.

'Morning, Laura.'

'I never thought I'd be so glad to see you,' she said.

'Something wrong?'

She grinned. 'Nothing personal. My horse pulled up lame.'

Wyatt swung down. 'Let's have a look at him.'

He stepped up to the horse, talking to it softly, bent and lifted the leg, carefully examining the hoof. He put it down, patting the animal. 'Split,' he said. 'He'll be all right but I'm afraid you'd better not ride him in.'

She considered him dubiously, pulled a lip between white teeth. 'It's a lucky thing you happened along.'

'Well,' Wyatt said, rasping his jaw, 'I didn't exactly happen along. I know you've been riding out here pretty often of a mornin'. Here, give me your hand; my pony can handle both of us. Be a pleasure to give you a lift back to town.'

She continued to study him, not moving, not saying anything either.

'Six miles,' he urged, 'is a right brisk walk in the heat of the day.' Then he grinned. 'I won't bite you.'

Her lips twisted faintly but her eyes were not altogether free of misgiving. Wyatt, tying the reins of her mount to his horn, swung up and reached down for her. She still did not appear entirely satisfied but six miles on shanks' mare was no salubrious prospect. She finally put out her hand and permitted Wyatt to swing her up behind him.

He didn't make the suggestion, but in this position she found herself compelled to put her arms about his chest. Or risk bouncing off. She naturally had no desire for a spill.

Wyatt grinned behind his mustache and put the horse up the ridge.

She camped hold of him more tightly, blushing, furiously aware of and considerably affected by the close proximity of their physical contact. 'Better keep a firm hold—' Wyatt's words floated back to her. 'This ground here's pretty rough.' Laura stretched

96

her arms a little farther around him. 'Tighter,' Wyatt called, and put the big roan into a canter.

She suspected he was grinning. She grinned reluctantly herself.

* * *

Charley Bassett, foot on fence, peered into the stockyards cattle pens. His reins-trailing horse stood hipshot beside him, desultorily flicking his ears at the flies. There was a mort of dust. Cowboys were hazing the stock into pens, tally men were counting, one of them tying knots in a rope, the other man setting little marks in a book. Several railroad men were looking on and cracking jokes. Doc Holliday appeared, coming up behind Wyatt's chief deputy. Charlie, sensing another presence, glanced over his shoulder, goggling as if he couldn't believe it. 'Heavens to Betsy! What's got you up at this time o' day? Why, it ain't hardly three o'clock yet!'

'All right, all right. Matter of fact, I'm on a health bender. Up before noon and take a twenty-yard cruise, regular as clockwork. This is the first day.' He glanced about, covering his nose with a handkerchief. 'Terrible lot of beef coming in. What'll they ever do with it all?'

'I guess someone'll eat it. This is just the beginning. You ain't seen nothin'. The really big herds'll be rollin' up soon.'

Doc took up a position alongside Charlie, both of them staring into the pens. Doc couldn't see enough of Charlie's face to gauge his expression. 'Where's Kate?' He practically had to shout to make himself heard above the cowboy yells and bawling steers.

Charlie Bassett scrinched a quick peek out of the corners of his eyes. Doc was still peering through the dust and bars trying to discover what was happening to all those horn-clacking cattle. While Bassett was fumbling around for words, not wanting to break it to Doc in a way that might turn the gambler's wrath upon him, Doc, twisting round, snarled, 'Where is she, man? Can't you understand plain English?'

'It's—well, it's kind of a touchy subjeck. I—' Bassett's lips fluttered like those of a female about to bury her head in an apron. He saw Doc sway toward him. He wanted to run. Doc's eyes laid hold of him like strangling fingers and twisted him around. He could feel his knees half push out from under him. Doc hawked loudly and spat. The bastard might as well have fired his pistol. Charlie choked back a sob. He began to sag.

Doc's eyes looked like fish scales. Old Charlie damn near fell down, he was that scared.

Where is she?

By God, he *had* drawn a gun! The snout of it was boring straight through Charlie's middle.

98

Bassett's arms flopped. His knees turned to rubber. 'Wiley's Hotel.' He couldn't seem to get it out quick enough now. 'Ringo's there. Kate's taken up with him.'

Doc turned slowly. He got his foot back up there onto the rail and kind of hunched over, staring into the pens again. After perhaps thirty seconds he said, 'What's the action here?'

Charlie, puzzled, tried to scrape himself together. 'We been collectin' their hardware fast as they hit town. Leastways we sure as hell been tryin'. Don't look like Bat's goin' to git back with our deppities . . . Doc, you just can't do it. A gunfight right now would bring old Wyatt a heap o' misery. Goddam it, it might even git him kilt! Can't you—'

'Sure is a lot of cattle,' Doc said. 'A mighty lot of cattle.'

* * *

But back in his room some ten minutes later the torment in Doc could no longer be hidden. Back and forth he paced like a cooped-up cougar. He whirled over to the dresser, stood for moments with fingers drumming against its dusty top. Impatient, he yanked open a drawer, got his shell belt off. Rolled about the holstered pistol he dropped it into the drawer, grimaced, and shut it.

About to turn he swung back. One hand

went out and fastened itself to the haft of a knife. He stood there, face working; flung the blade viciously into the wall. He was in a hell of a temper as he walked across the room and yanked the knife free.

*   *   *

It was night again and full dark now with Front Street stippled in light and shadow. There was plenty of business and noise and whooping as the crew from the herd, hard cash in their pockets, set out to catch up on things too long denied them. Doc looked neither to right nor left. Like the tracks he rolled down the middle of the street in his black frock coat and gambler's string tie until he came to the DEADLINE sign and crossed over, deliberately moving onto the south walk.

He pulled in his stride to move slower now, peering into the shabby, cheap rundown dens of vice and iniquity, out of many of which issued roars of laughter, drunken talk, maudlin songs, fiddles' screech, the tinpanny clang of out-of-tune pianos. From some, nickelodeons ground out their tunes, from others came wrangling, shouts and curses. Their lights flicked across him, briefly illumining that cold and set face. At one point a drunk came reeling out onto the walk. At another the gambler stepped over a prostrate body. A girl swept up to him, mouthing endearments, caught a gleam in his eyes and backed away. Now and again someone, recognizing him, stopped dead in his tracks.

Doc went on like the march of doom.

Like the wrath of God he passed Wiley's Hangtree Gambling Hall, boots banging out a hollow thunder from the planks that rattled and sometimes gave with his step. Now he stood stopped before Wiley's Hotel. There was not so much noise here and very little light.

He stepped into a lobby that was cavernous with shadows. A solitary lamp, its wick turned low, burned untended on a counter beside an open book.

Doc entered a hallway where the distant sound of a ragtime piano grew as faint in the gloom as the frightened beat of a moth's fluttering wings. There was no light here but that seeping out from behind closed doors. Doc studied the doors, moving catfooted now. He found one that he appeared to favor and paused a long moment to crouch there eyeing it. The sound of feet came up behind him. A dancehall girl with a laughing cowhand turned into a room just across the way.

Doc, finally stirring, moved up to the door he'd been so steadily watching. He put out a hand as though to knock, decided against it and twisted the knob. The door swung back and Doc was into the room.

A lamp showed Kate on a couch, drink in hand. Between couch and door was a grimy table with a dozen bottles on it.

'What are you doing in this dump?' Doc growled.

'Well, well!' Kate laughed. 'If it isn't the little deputy.'

'I certainly called the turn on you. A goddam whore, bed an' all! You're every last thing I named you—taking up with a crazy gunman like Ringo. Or maybe,' Doc said, 'you've got something in mind—something having to do with Wyatt.'

'What the hell difference does it make to you where I go or who I take up with?' Her red lips writhed into a belligerent sneer. 'Maybe I do have something in mind.'

Doc's contemptuous stare let go of her and moved to Ringo standing with gun half drawn in another door.

'If you're nixing to use that hogleg,' Doc said, 'use it.'

Ringo snarled. 'You got no right to come bustin' in here—'

'I do what I please, whenever I please, where I please.'

'You'd look good with your neck folded over a crate top, with your shiny boots flopped from its bottom. Now get the hell out—'

'I came to see Kate. We've got some talking to do.'

'Anything you got to say,' Kate sneered, 'you can say in front of him.'

Doc's burning eyes whipped back to her. 'I

guess I've said it all. You slut.'

He turned to go.

'Just a minute,' Ringo growled, coming forward. 'You don't talk to my woman like that—'

'Save your blather. You can have your cheap whore.'

'By God, I'm goin' to blast you apart!'

'I don't have a gun.'

'Ain't you the brave one!' Ringo holstered the gun that was in his hand and, catching hold of its mate, lifted it out of his belt and slid it over the table where it stopped on the edge, scant inches from Doc's hand.

'You got one now,' Ringo said.

Doc smiled coldly. Ignoring the pistol he reached up to rub at his neck. 'I'm not fighting.'

Ringo laughed, eyes jeering. Doc reddened. Doc's fingers squirmed.

'Go on,' Ringo said. 'Grab it.'

When Doc just stood there the gunfighter guffawed. 'The terrible Doc Holliday!' He laughed uproariously.

Kate said, 'He won't fight. He promised Wyatt Earp to be a sweet little boy.'

'I always figured,' Ringo said, 'you made that rep putting away a bunch of drunks.' His lips curled back. 'You're a yellow skunk.'

Doc's hand inched toward the back of his collar.

'Watch him!' Kate screamed.

Ringo backed away a couple steps. Then he snorted. 'No more harm in him than a chambermaid. An old maid could chase him with a bundle of shucks. Have a drink, Holliday. Mebbe it'll put some backbone into you.'

Picking up a glass half filled with whisky he dashed the contents into Doc's face.

Though he went stiff as a ramrod and white as chalk, Doc made no move. He gave Kate a long look, then turned and walked out. Ringo gaped, then doubled over with laughter. Kate ran to the door and fell against it, sobbing.

'Oh, Doc—Doc—' she cried in a whisper. She spun about. 'Shut up, you ape!'

Doc stood trembling with rage in the hall. Through the door he could hear the continued guffaws of Ringo. He shook as with an ague. Seething, face contorted, he stomped into the lobby and out onto the street.

CHAPTER EIGHT

This was a gala night at the Dodge House. A banner stretched over the side door read: DANCE AND CHURCH BAZAAR. Gay strains of music floated over the environs. There were a lot of folks catching their breath on the verandah, the ladies waggling their fans, the gents attempting with fingers to stretch

104

too-tight collars, as Mayor Kelly and Laura stepped out for a moment.

At the nearby intersection a shay was pulled up in the gloom of box elders, Wyatt impatiently fiddling with the reins. He'd been watching the exits for almost a half hour. On seeing Laura he hauled in the weight, picked up the whip and got ready to move. But Laura hadn't yet departed from Kelly. 'It's a lovely dance; I'm truly sorry to have to be running off so soon.'

'The floor,' Kelly said, on an outgoing breath, 'will be covered with busted hearts.'

Laura laughed. 'Good night, Mayor.'

She came over the street and stepped up on the walk. She seemed to move slowly passing Wyatt's office, at least till she discovered the head-tipped shape with his boots on the desk could not possibly be the marshal. Just as she reached the intersection. Wyatt's shay drove up beside her. The marshal jumped out.

'Evenin', Laura. Can I give you a lift?'

'What—again? I guess not.' She smiled. 'For such a short way I believe the walk will do me good. I seem to be inclined to eat more than I can afford.'

She started to turn away, but Wyatt wouldn't leave it there. 'It's early,' he urged. 'I've got to ride out to the bluffs. Thought you might care to keep me company.'

'Thanks, but I have to get home.'

105

'You're an expert on percentages. Let's analyze the situation.'

'What situation?'

'The lady gambler who has convinced the town she's completely untouchable and the poor but honest marshal who's convinced despite all evidence that under her grand manners is a heart that beats in a real she-male woman.'

'Wyatt, I'm *not* about to ride out of town with you.'

'Why not? You're a gambler. You know all the odds. It isn't as though you had anything to fear. Everyone will tell you I'm devout, righteous and completely dedicated to my work. In fact, I believe you said as much yourself. Now who in the world could you be safer with?'

She was plainly intrigued, but oddly nervous, too. After studying him a moment she said, 'I suppose the bluffs at night *are* rather splendid—if there were light enough out there to see anything.'

'Oh, there is,' he assured her. 'We might even hear a coyote howl.'

'If you're sure there aren't any wolves around?' She reached out her hand.

Wyatt lost no time helping her into the vehicle. He hadn't really expected so much luck. He climbed in after her and got the horse moving.

The bluffs were only a few miles out of

Dodge and in the daytime presented a rather exciting view of the town and the rolling country that lay roundabout it. There wasn't any moon, but driving along the bluffs on the old dirt road one did catch a pretty stimulating view, what with all the lights of the town spread out like a glimmer of jewels against black velvet.

'It's beautiful,' Laura said. 'I'm glad you persuaded me to come. I hadn't realized Dodge had grown so much these last weeks.'

Wyatt stopped the rig, wrapped the reins about the whipstock. 'Want to step down and walk a bit?'

'Well—just a little,' she said dubiously.

He lifted her down.

'You're very strong, Marshal.'

'You don't need to look so scared,' he said.

'I'm not scared. Not really.'

'All right,' he said. 'Now tell me why you came.'

She tipped her head, watching him. 'I've been wondering what makes a man like you tick. I've been wondering about you ever since that evening you arrested me in Dodge—watching you drive yourself and the men around you, walking into terrible danger every moment you're on duty. I've wondered if what everyone says is really true.'

'What do they say?'

'They say you're not a man but a machine—a 'killing' machine. I don't very often let myself

107

get curious about people, but I have to admit to being curious about you. Are you human, Mr. Earp? Or are you just a trigger finger?'

He caught her to him and kissed her fiercely. At first she struggled to break the embrace, then relaxed against him, eyes big as teacups. When he turned her loose she drew back, puzzled and half frightened.

'Doesn't that answer your question?'

'Oh, Wyatt . . . Wyatt . . .'

He brought her into his arms again, her own coming up to close about his neck. His lips closed on hers and she came fully against him. How long this went on neither one of them knew but suddenly, gasping, she broke away. She moved blindly off a few steps, panting. He came up behind her. She said, 'We'd better stop this.'

He grasped her shoulders, forcing her to face him. 'No, Wyatt, no!'

'Who's the one that's not human? Stop making yourself unreachable. You've got a heart. Why not listen to it?'

'There's nothing in this for me,' she said. 'You're a legalized gunslinger. I'm not going to end up like Kate Fisher.'

'Laura. Good Lord, I want to marry you!'

'I can't understand that. You hardly know me.'

'But well enough to know I love you.'

She slipped out of his hands. 'It wouldn't work, Wyatt. I'm not falling in love with any badge toter.'

'But I wouldn't be a badge toter all my life. We could start a ranch—'

'You haven't a life to share. Your life belongs to the law. I've seen too many marshals' wives dry up and wither away before their time. You're Wyatt Earp, the iron marshal. You'll never be anything else—I wouldn't want you to.'

'I could be anything you wanted me to be,' Wyatt said earnestly. 'We'll buy some cows—'

'No,' Laura said with considerable emphasis. 'My mother had cows and so did my sister. I told you about them.'

'But if we want each other . . . Lord, there's plenty of other work I could take up.'

'Is there? No, Wyatt.' She shook her head. 'You'll never get away from your reputation. Wherever you go there'll be a badge and a gun.'

He dropped his arms. 'I expect you're not much of a gambler, after all.' He pulled himself together. 'Let's get on back to town.'

*   *   *

Front street appeared deserted. In front of the Marshal's Office Charlie Bassett lounged with his shoulders braced against a post, humming somewhat off-key a dancehall tune called the Cuckoo Song in time with the music coming out of the Dodge House. Charlie tapped one foot and then tapped the other.

There was nothing rowdy about the Dodge House. Everything there moved with utmost decorum as befitted a church sociable. Take that table with the punch bowl—real punch, no spikes. The platform was provided with a fiddle, a banjo and a piano and three sweating men who were top hands at making them talk. All about the sides of the room little knots of people were engaged with their various conversations and, out on the floor in embraces of varying closeness, about twelve couples were doing the Little Foot. A group of the town's leading citizens, mostly merchants, were gathered off to one side about the corpulent shape of the Dodge City mayor. Right in the midst of the most earnest part of whatever it was that Kelly had on his mind a racket of gunfire shook the room's windows. A gabble of yells burst out of the street and chin music, band music, and everything else including the mayor, came to a stop in a kind of stunned silence.

Charlie Bassett flew jangling into the room. 'It's that long-legged, fat-assed sonofabitch, Pierce! His crew has treed Front Street. No one's to step outside of this room. I mean that!' He caught Kelly's eye and the mayor waddled over. Bassett said, 'Climb out a back window an' try to find Earp. Go on—get a wiggle on! I'll do what I can to keep them in hand.'

110

Outside it was pretty bad, sure enough. Through the wind and dust and the Rebel yells twenty-five big-hatted horsebackers flourishing pistols were filling the street with a bedlam of shouting, riding their horses up and down the walks and some of them even into places of business, shooting out windows, roping stovepipes and going skallyhooting off with them, and otherwise acting like a bunch of wild Indians, while a trio of others, non-participants, lounged in their saddles enjoying this frivolity. One of these was Johnny Ringo, mean, vindictive and full of rotgut. The larger of the other pair who were taking this in with a vast satisfaction was Pierce himself—old Abel Head Pierce, better known as 'Shanghai,' the Rhode Island-born son of a blacksmith who had come into Texas at the age of nineteen and got into the cattle business through the back door by building a fence. He was an extremely loud talker and frequently given to exaggeration. He was also tight fisted and seldom forgot an injury and at this particular time of his life he was at the height of his arrogance as a Texas cattle king, wealthy, powerful, and bossing a tough crew. He had a foot-long cigar poled through his fat lips and both his saddle and gear blazed with silver.

'Lively bunch—eh, Ringo?' he said, and back-handed the gunfighter unexpectedly in the belly, laughing uproariously at the man's pained expression.

111

'Yeah,' Ringo managed to grunt somewhat feebly.

'Can't you show a little enthusiasm?' Shanghai demanded, vigorously puffing his cigar. 'This here oughta learn them once an' fer all who owns the cowtowns, don't you reckon?'

Ringo spat and said 'Yeah,' and looked like for two cents he'd blow the big auger plumb loose of his saddle.

Amid the dust and the confusion of all that yelling and horsing around, Shanghai's foreman—the other gent sitting there—spied Bassett approaching from out of an alley. He didn't know who this was but had caught the glint of the badge on his vest and, lifting out his sixshooter, laid the long-barreled weapon ready for service across the knobs of his drawn-up knees.

Bassett, stomping out of the dust, yelled. 'Call them fools off before somebody gits hurt!'

'Who the hell are you?' Shanghai roared.

'I'm the deppity marshal.'

'You go tell your boss I'm not about to settle fer anythin' less'n his personal attention.'

'By Gawd, I'm puttin' you under arrest, Pierce!'

Shanghai laughed. 'You hear that, Ringo? I'm under arrest.'

'Yeah,' Ringo said, and put a gob of tobacco juice within an inch of Bassett's boot.

112

The deputy marshal caught hold of Shanghai's coat. Ringo's hands dropped over his gun butts. There was a noticeable tightening of the supercharged air; then Bassett, swearing, went for his gun. Two reports cracked out before Bassett cleared leather. Charlie staggered, arms flopping, backed a few hurried steps and went down like a log.

*   *   *

In the back room room at the Long Branch, Cockeyed Frank Loving, dealing faro, put his head to one side in an attitude of listening.

Doc, looking up, rubbed the back of his neck. 'Reminds me of hell emigrating on cart wheels.'

'What say we quit? I'd like to get out there.'

'Frank, my boy, just keep passing those pasteboards. I'm not breaking this run.'

Half a dozen slugs crashed into the room. Great shards fell out of the room's single window and a nude lady in a frame resting against the far wall suddenly became endowed with a second belly button that went all the way through her like the tunnel of a mine. A bottle shattered on a table by Doc's left elbow. Loving's face turned livid. Doc, never turning a hair, eyed his cards.

'For Chrissake, Doc!'

'Deal.'

Back at the church sociable in the ballroom

113

of the Dodge House, everyone but the piano thumper was huddled in a corner with the shaking women. A great and pervading quiet appeared to be spreading over the street outside. Some of Pierce's crew came stumbling through the doors, wild-eyed and powdered with trail dust. Shanghai tramped in with Ringo and his cold-jawed foreman.

'Well,' Pierce said, 'What've we got here? Look back there, Johnnie. I'd say some of them jaspers has been havin' a hoedown. You wanta dance with them hoors, boys?'

Shocked gasps flew up from the outraged gathering. Pierce put on a scowl. His foreman said, 'This ain't a very hospitable outfit. Mebbe we ought to learn them some manners.'

A merchant said from a group at one side, 'Better get those bums of yours south of the deadline.'

Shanghai roared, 'You hear that, boys? These here bluenoses don't appreciate friendliness. We ain't good enough for 'em! They like our money but don't figure we're fit to take hold of their women.'

Several of his whiskered trail hands grinned. One fellow yanked out a sixshooter and brought down a lamp in a cascade of oil and shattered glass. The rest of them whooped like a bunch of Comanches.

Shanghai dug out his own cannon then. He put a couple of slugs above the piano man's

114

fingers. 'Strike up a tune!'

With the command, Pierce's crew bolted for the heifers. Several of the crowd made an effort to interfere and were promptly knocked sprawling. Ringo and Pierce's foreman covered the crowd with their pistols while his crew seized the women and, dragging them out into the cleared center of the hall, began to wrestle them about more as though they were steers than anything human. The man at the piano pounded out the Sailor's Hornpipe. Two of the trail hands, dancing in rapt togetherness, burst suddenly apart and started pummeling each other.

The fight swiftly spread, sweeping over the bandstand as the pair's compadres joined the melee with an assortment of whoops and swear words. The banjo picker and the violinist leaped incontinently from the platform, abandoning their instruments, digging for the tules. In less time than it takes to relate, the banjo became a shortlived club and some unfortunate shopkeeper with blood and deep scratches on the sides of his face went howling from the shambles in a froth of splinters and fiddle strings.

One trail hand got knocked into the punch bowl and sat there grinning from ear to ear. A horse charged snorting and squealing through the carnage, the cowboy astride him catapulting from his back in a flying leap for the chandelier which came down like the walls of Jericho. All this while the pale piano pounder's nicotine-stained fingers had been flying over the keys like a bat out of Carlsbad. But now, in the very midst of *Miss Mulligan's Piano-Fortay*, the ivories went astonishingly still with the effect of a Fall River factory shutting down. All over the room there was a hiatus in the racket as men and even the ladies—what was left of them—paused to catch second wind and exchange bewildered looks with those nearest.

As ripples spread out across rocked waters the vortex of the hush appeared to be thickest about the main entrance and the reason for this was pretty soon apparent as increasing numbers of those present discovered Marshal Wyatt Earp standing there with a rifle.

The fool in the punch bowl clambered out and stood shamefacedly dripping while the rest of his outfit, cautiously shifting, took up a stand behind Shanghai and Ringo as the women took refuge in the arms of their men. Neither moving nor speaking, Wyatt stood like something hacked out of stone, the hot glare of his eyes ominously fastened on Pierce. Shanghai himself looked like some lout of a kid caught with both paws in the cash box. His long neck turned red and he swelled up like a carbuncle. 'I thought this would pull you out of your hide hole! Now, you goddam gun-whackin' sonofabitch, you're goin' to pay up with interest fer this scar you give me in

Wichita!'

Wyatt said, whisper-soft, 'If you varmints are itchin' for a real jamboree I may only get two or three of you, but the first one down is going to be Pierce. Get out of those shell belts an' belly up to the wall. Anybody I see with a gun in his fist will sure as hell get it broken. Start peelin'.'

'You better start prayin',' Shanghai blustered. 'You've pulled your last bluff!'

And Ringo chipped in, 'He sure has, Boss. Let's work him over.'

But it was all too apparent that none of the rest of them thought Earp was bluffing. Belts and pistols were dropping all over like a flight of tired geese coming down for water. Then, just when it looked as though the frolic was over, Pierce's foreman palmed up his cutter and started blowing out the lamps. 'Take him, boys!' Pierce yelled, and the whole crew surged forward with a howl, grabbing up their weapons.

But the avalanche stopped as if it had hit a stone wall when dapper Doc Holliday with a gun in each fist stepped through the side door. He didn't have to say a word. One look at the killer blaze of his stare was enough to take the starch from pretty near anything. Doc grinned like a wolf and the guns dropped out of their fists in a hurry.

But not all of them. Pierce still had his and, with his eyes shuttling back and forth between

Earp and Holliday, he looked like a man who was plumb hankering to use it. Ringo, still armed, growled, 'Call the play, Shanghai,' and Pierce's cold jawed foreman said, 'We kin take them buggers!'

'But you'll get it first, Shanghai,' Wyatt said stonily. 'They will be scrapin' up your pieces all over Ford County.'

Doc bored in on the flank. Those nearest fell back before his advance. You could smell the death on him, you could see it in his face. He stopped about ten yards away from Wyatt.

Pierce didn't know what to do. He'd been waiting a long while for a chance to cut Wyatt down, but he sure wasn't craving to die in the process. The muzzle of Wyatt's rifle was leveled straight at his brisket.

'You may get me,' Wyatt said quietly, 'but if you don't unbuckle inside of five seconds there's goin' to be a double funeral, and I'm starting the count now. One ... two ... three ...'

Sweat popped out all over Pierce's face. That goddam Earp would just as lief do it. He said like he was talking through a mouthful of worms, 'You heard him, boys. Throw down your irons.'

Doc laughed nastily. 'First sensible thing you ever said.'

There was a halfhearted grumble of protest from those of the crew who were not directly in the immediate line of fire. Wyatt paid no attention to this face-saving gesture. He stepped forward, the snout of his gunbarrel not ten inches from Shanghai's paunch.

More guns dropped. But Ringo, thinking he saw a chance, tipped his up. A blast from Doc tore the weapon from his fingers and he spun onto his knees clutching a shattered arm.

'Anybody else feel lucky?' Doc asked.

'Scrape him up,' Wyatt said, 'an' let's move.'

Shanghai and his foreman pulled Ringo onto his feet. The gunfighter snarled, 'You ain't heard the last of this, Holliday!'

'That's because I'm in a charitable mood.'

Pierce and his gangling foreman, half supporting the cursing Ringo between them, led the way to the street, the sullen crew straggling after them under the guns of Doc and Earp. At the door Wyatt turned, 'Anybody hurt here?'

Several of the least cowed townsmen shook their heads. 'We're all right,' one of the merchants said.

'Somebody get a doctor for Charlie Bassett. A couple of you boys pick up that hardware and bring it over to the jail. The rest had better go home. We'll hold court on this business first thing tomorrow morning. I want all of you there.'

As Wyatt came into the street it appeared that Doc had things well under control. No one was giving him any trouble. 'I guess,' Wyatt said, 'you don't want my thanks.'

'Can I put thanks in my pocket? Will it get me back that good run of luck? Let's just say the account is paid in full.'

Wyatt said, 'That suits me fine.' He looked at Pierce's outfit. 'All right, get going. You'll find the jail straight ahead.'

*   *   *

Some time later, with all the drovers locked up, Wyatt, at an open shed stable behind the Dodge House, went through the business of bedding down his horse. Just as he started away from the place Laura's voice came worriedly out of the shadows.

'Wyatt?'

'I'm all right,' Wyatt said.

She came against him. 'Oh, Wyatt—'

'What are you shaking for? Good lord, girl—'

'I was so frightened. I've never been so scared in my life. What if you'd been killed?'

'Would you have cared?'

Her arms tightened. 'Everything's changed. All my values have gone topsy turvy. I don't seem even to know my own mind any more. I don't know what's wrong or what's right—and I don't care.'

CHAPTER NINE

The next day when Wyatt stepped into the Long Branch Saloon on his rounds he found Doc alone at a table, hardly yet well started on his afternoon whisky. Wyatt said, 'How's tricks, Doc?'

'Pretty tricky.' Doc scowled.

Wyatt dropped into a chair. 'Just thought you might like to know,' he said smiling, 'there's about to be one less star-packer around here.'

'Charlie worse?' Doc asked, looking up.

'Charlie's all right.'

Doc peered at him quizzically. 'So you're turnin' in the tin.'

'Heading for Californy,' Wyatt said. 'Going to try ranching. I've decided to take that good advice you were passing out a while back and get out of this business before I turn into another Cotton Wilson.'

'Smart man.'

'Laura's coming with me. We're going to travel in double harness. Would you like to congratulate the prospective groom?'

'She's a lady,' Doc said. This, coming from him, was quite a testimonial.

'We'd take it kindly if you could see fit to come to the wedding. That is, if it won't take you away too long from your poker game.'

Doc delicately hoisted his whisky, grunted unintelligibly and tossed down the slug. 'Deal me out,' he said, putting the glass down.' My forte is funerals. I'd be no good to you there.'

Wyatt stood up. 'Well,' Doc sighed, 'good luck to both of you. You're smart to be getting out of this country.'

'Why don't you try your luck down the road?'

Doc shook his head. He poured himself another whisky.

*   *   *

Later, up in his room at the Dodge House, Doc wearily sat down and stretched out on his bed. Kate came in without knocking and put her back to the window. Her face showed lines of dissipation and weariness went deep into her. Doc didn't even bother to get up.

Lips trembling, she said hardly louder than a kind of forlorn whisper, 'Doc, for God's sake, take me back!'

'No.'

'Please. I'll do anything—anything you say. I don't care how you treat me.'

Doc, getting up, went over to the dresser, leaning on it, head hung over like a beat-out horse, with his back about all Kate could get a good look at.

'Give me another chance,' she pleaded, only one blink away from tears.

Doc swung around and faced her. 'I never gave you much of a chance. But I'm not blaming you, either, not for anything, Kate. Maybe—maybe it could have been different if I'd been right for you in the first place. But we can't turn back the clock—'

'It ain't too late. I'll be good to you, Doc. I swear it!'

She rushed over, intending to fling her arms around him, but he pushed her away. 'It's too late for the both of us. Do something better for yourself while you can.'

Kate, openly begging, said, 'Doc—Doc—don't let me go back there.'

Holliday turned away as though exhausted. 'Go,' he sighed. 'Just leave me alone.'

Color sprang into Kate's face. Her eyes flashed. 'I'll see you dead!' And she went storming out, the door slamming behind her.

Doc reeled over to the bed and fell onto it.

*   *   *

At the Marshal's Office Wyatt, cleaning out his desk, was throwing things into the trash can, practically everything he figured to have no further use for. A clean sweep, he told himself, nodding and whistling.

Charlie Bassett came in with his arm in a sling. Wyatt eyed him and grunted but, not seeing the telegram Charlie was carrying, paid him no particular attention. Chances are, in his present frame of mind—all perked up with the thoughts of the future he envisioned with Laura—he would not even have noticed had Charlie stuck a gun in his face. He went blithely on, throwing away old dodgers and whatnot.

Dumping a pile of records, he said, 'These are all dead ducks, Charlie; no use clutterin' the place up with 'em. But these,' he grinned, tossing a handful of expense vouchers across to the deputy, 'I guess you'll be finding a use for. Every time you step out to the backhouse the Council will expect to get one of these from you.'

He sent his marshal's badge spinning across the desk. 'That's yours, too. Keep a good shine on it. Well,' he grinned, slamming shut the empty drawers, 'I guess that winds me up as a lawman. For good, I hope.'

Bassett's continued silence appeared abruptly to register with Wyatt. His head came up, wheeled around. He stared for a long still moment at the disturbed expression on Charlie's face. Then he saw the telegram and stretched out his hand. Bassett pushed it across the desk.

He tore open the envelope, peered at Charlie again, and dropped his glance to the lines of type. His jaw turned grim as the message got home to him.

Out on the bluffs Laura said, some time later, 'I should have known you couldn't quit.

Something like this was bound to happen.'

They were standing under the big tree near *their* wash, their horses behind them on dragging reins munching at whatever grass they could find.

'Laura, please. After all, Virgil's my brother. He's in trouble. He needs me. Is that too much to understand?'

'I understand I've been rather foolish to have imagined you could ever love anyone. Go if you must. I won't stand in your way. But we're not going to start anything at all as long as you've got a gun in your hand.'

'But, honey—'

'What makes you feel he needs you more than I do?' Her lips firmed, her chin came up. 'It's your choice, Wyatt. Either you cut clean away from—'

'Or what?' he said, frowning.

'I've given up my way of life for you. I told you when we first met, right here on this very spot, I wouldn't follow you from town to town—sitting in the dark, expecting every moment someone to come riding out with news that you've been killed. I won't do it, Wyatt. If your love isn't strong enough—'

'I'll swear I'll never touch a gun again after Tombstone.'

'You'll never be through with it. Your reputation will find you wherever we are.'

'But Laura, this is my brother!'

'And I'm the girl you were going to marry. If

125

your brother means more to you than a wife—'

'That's not fair!'

'It's as fair as what you're proposing to do.'

'Don't ask me to let Virg down.'

'But it's all right to let *me* down. Is that it?' she said sharply. 'I told you once no man would ever get me to pull a plow. Those were pretty empty words, I guess. I'd give up anything—go anyplace for you. I'll face anything with you, except a gun. You've got to meet me halfway, Wyatt.'

He said, barely breathing, 'I've got to go to Virg.'

'Then go!' she cried. 'Clean up Tombstone! There's a hundred tough towns on the frontier practically begging for the great Wyatt Earp. Go ahead—clean them all up.'

She turned her back on him, stood there shaking. Coming up behind her he softly kissed her neck, but she stood there stifly, completely withdrawn from him.

'I love you,' he said, and let his hands drop tiredly. He looked at her a moment and, sighing, went over and caught up the reins of his horse, pulled himself into the saddle and rode off up the road in the direction of town.

There was anguish in Laura's face as she stared after him. She half lifted a hand but, even with the tears, her chin stayed up. She would not let herself call him back.

*   *   *

On the road from Dodge City that same afternoon, in the dust and glare and rattle of wheels, an Army caisson slowly crept through the heat.

Wyatt, a weary and saddened man lost in bleak thoughts, was hunched over the driver's seat listlessly holding the reins in gloved hands.

Behind him a horseman was hurrying to catch up. Not until he'd yelled half a dozen times did Wyatt come out of his brooding and pull up. He must have recognized Doc but his expression held no particular interest and, certainly, no curiosity.

'Afternoon, Marshal,' the gambler grinned, reining in. 'You just out for the ride?'

'About seven hundred miles' worth.'

'Tombstone, eh? A remarkable coincidence,' Doc said dryly, lighting up one of the crooked stogies he favored. 'I was heading that way myself. Thought the climate down there might be better for my cough.'

'At least you won't have so far to go when you leave. Never knew you to be interested in your health. What is this, something recent?'

'Well,' Doc said, rasping a hand along his jaw, 'to tell you the truth, it's a matter of finances mostly. Nobody will give me any play around Dodge; I haven't any choice in the matter. It's move or starve. I don't suppose— even if I still had those nags—I could sell them back to Shanssey for anything like what he

127

charged me for them. Took my whole roll,' he said with a parched grin. 'Twenty grand. Still, he wasn't a bad coot. Mind if I ride along?'

'It's a free range, they tell me.' Wyatt sighed. 'Where's your gear?'

Doc, taking a deck of cards from his pocket, held them up. Then he got off his horse, twisted the reins about the horn, headed him for town and slapped him on the rump. He climbed into the empty half of Wyatt's seat. Wyatt joggled the lines and the wagon moved on.

'Be a dry ride,' he said presently.

Doc had taken off his coat. He reached back now and got a bottle from the pocket. He exchanged a look with Wyatt. Both men grinned.

The days slipped past.

About the middle of an unusually warm afternoon as they were traveling through a region of gray shale ridges, deep cutbanks and stony outcrops festooned with wolf's candle and Spanish dagger, Wyatt staring off across that gray haze of baked rock, remarked, 'Another town up ahead.'

Doc scrinched his eyes against the glare. 'I don't see it,' he said irritably.

'Over there,' Wyatt grunted. 'On top of that mesa. Don't you see those mine hoists?'

'I'll take your word for it.'

'Where there's mines,' Earp said, 'there ought to be money. And where there's money

128

there'll be people.'

'Never knew it to fail.' Doc waved a hand. 'There's a hell's smear of cartridge cases strewed along the sides of this road.'

'There's a rusted six-shooter,' Wyatt said, pointing.

'And a rifle without any stock,' Doc added. 'You reckon this is the place?'

'Looks enough like it from what Virg said.'

'Well, we'll know when we get there.'

Wyatt pulled up after a bit and sat stiffly listening. 'Sounded like shots.'

Doc said irascibly, 'Them cartridge cases don't just grow there.'

They went on, steadily climbing, gusts of wind whipped up out of the gullies blowing hotter and rougher through the gray immensity of baked desolation. Doc growled presently, 'You ever see the beat of this? Must be the back door to hell. Even the goddam creosote bushes ain't hardly bigger than burro weeds. If this is Tombstone she's rightly named.'

They came out of their climb on the brow of a hill that was studded with headboards and whitewashed wooden crosses, both of them bearded and grimy and haggard. Doc, peering around, had a bad coughing spell. 'Boot Hill,' he croaked when he got back his breath. 'We've come seven hundred miles to reach a land of gray rock and corpses!'

They saw the town spread out ahead of

129

them. 'Must be three thousand people still unplanted around these diggings,' Wyatt said.

'Well, there's still a mite of room on that hill,' Doc said dryly.

Wyatt drove on. Doc said suddenly, 'You know, by God, I feel cooler. Breathe better, too. How high do you reckon we are?'

'About as near to heaven as we're likely to get.' Wyatt pointed out a sign that read O.K. CORRAL. 'Want to pull up there?'

'Let's drive on a ways.'

Wyatt pointed down a side street. 'There's the Wells-Fargo office.'

'I'll try the tables first.'

Wyatt's mouth tightened somewhat but he kept his thoughts to himself. He pulled over to the side, pulled around in a wide circle and stopped the wagon in front of an old man lounging against the fence. He looked like a stable hand and talked as if he had stock in the local Chamber.

'Welcome to Tombstone, gents,' he hailed, straightening up. 'You're a-standin' right now on the very spot where Curly Bill downed Marshal Fred White. Yes, sir—biggest town in the entire Southwest. Bar none. You figger to be here long?'

'We'll be around for a spell,' Wyatt said, getting down with a noticeable stiffness. 'Put these horses and wagon up for sale. We want a fair price.'

Doc, peering around, said, 'Where's a

decent hotel?'

'Next street down.' The ancient waved. 'Cosmopolitan—absolutely first class. None finer. I'll fetch a buckboard an' take your gear over.'

'Where at,' Wyatt said, 'does Virgil Earp live?'

'The marshal? Straight down Fremont Street. That's this 'un, right back the way you come. Can't miss it. On the corner of First—only house there.' He peered at them curiously. 'Don't believe I caught your name.'

'Didn't throw it.' Wyatt gave Doc a wave of the hand. 'Be seeing you around,' he said, and tramped stiff-legged off, following the toothless gabber's directions.

PART THREE

TOMBSTONE

CHAPTER TEN

In the Virgil Earp kitchen Wyatt sat at table with his assembled brothers, Morgan, Virgil and James, swallowing the last few mouthfuls of a bang-up dinner. It was full dark out now. In the light of the coal-oil lamps Betty (Virgil's wife), cleaning off the plates, looked about eight months gone with child. Tommy Earp, age four, was ensconsed on Wyatt's knee.

'Lordy,' Wyatt exclaimed, passing a hand across the tightness of his belt. 'That was the best assortment of groceries my stomach's got hold of in more time than I care to think back on. I'd just about forgot a home-cooked meal could be that good.'

He slipped an affectionate hand about Betty's waist. 'I think I'll have to steal you from Virg.'

'By golly, Wyatt,' Morgan said after the laugh, 'you're goin' to be the only bachelor Earp left in the tribe. I got a family goin' in Deadwood an' even little Jimmy here is tyin' the knot quick's he can git back to Californy.'

James Earp said indignantly, 'What do you mean, 'little' Jimmy? I'll be nineteen next month.'

Betty, rumpling his hair, said, 'You'd better be having a man-to-man talk with your brothers.'

135

James blushed. 'I know a heap more'n you figger I do.'

They all laughed again.

Morgan said, 'When are you fixin' to get hitched, Wyatt?'

Wyatt, frowning, shook his head. 'I don't know,' he sighed on an outgoing breath. The silence got a little uncomfortable. Betty lugged off an armload of dishes to the sink. Virgil drummed his fingers on the table.

Betty, looking back, said, 'I guess it's time for the women and kids to run out and play. Come along, Tommy. As a matter of fact, it's high time you were in bed.'

'Aw, Mom. Do I got to?'

'Come along. Your uncles will all be here tomorrow.'

'Good night, Uncle Wyatt.'

'Good night, Deputy.'

Tommy said good night to the others and his father kissed him. Reluctantly the lad took hold of his mother's hand. As they were going through the door, Betty said over her shoulder, 'it was mighty nice of you to come. I—I only wish it were under pleasanter circumstances.'

'Seems pretty upset.' Morgan said when she was gone.

'It's the pregnancy.' Virgil frowned. 'She's all the time after me to give up the badge. Hell, you know how women are. Any of you boys want cigars?'

They all lighted up, the older three

136

watching with some amusement as James, the youngest, got his going and vigorously puffed on it. But soon, he surreptitiously set it aside. 'Think I'll go out and take a look at the horses,' he said.

Virgil said, 'Morg an' Jim know the setup here. The whole trouble's them Clantons,' he told Wyatt. 'You know, Ike has a ranch outside the city limits. Got the toughest bunch of gunslingers for a crew you ever laid eyes on. Been rustling Mexican cattle, an' he owns the county sheriff.'

'Who's that?' said Wyatt.

'Old friend of yours—Cotton Wilson.'

'He's here?'

'Yep, an' sittin' pretty as a hawg on ice.'

'I tell you,' Virgil growled, 'we was sure-enough sick when we found Ike owned him, lock, stock an' barrel. Boils down to this: Clanton's runnin' wild in the county and Cotton is protectin' him. He's got a ranchful of Mex'kin cattle and he's sure as hell got to move 'em. Handiest place he can ship from is Tombstone. You see where that leaves us? He can't realize a nickel so long as we control the town.'

'That's about the size of it,' Morgan agreed. 'The bastard's organized, and he's mean. We can't keep him out of this town forever—not without we get help. That's why we sent for you.'

Wyatt said, 'What about these people

137

around here? They stand back of you?'

'John Clum will, anyway. He was Apache Agent here. Now he edits and publishes *The Epitaph*, Tombstone's paper. Some of the other city fathers will probably swing in line once they know you're callin' the shots.'

'We've all agreed,' Jimmy said, rejoining them still somewhat green about the gills, 'you're to ramrod this go-around.'

'One thing,' Morgan said, 'that bothers me, and I'll get it off my chest right now. That's this: there'll be a mort of gabble about you ridin' with Doc Holliday.'

Wyatt stiffened and set his jaw but Morgan went on doggedly. 'He's about the worst damn killer on the whole frontier. I had to run him out of Deadwood account of him borin' a couple of prominent citizens. It don't look good, him comin' here with you.'

'The straight of it is Doc saved my bacon in Dodge, and more than once. I can't go back on that. Also, in spite of his faults, he's a man of his word. He's got a place here, boys, so long as he deals straight and keeps his gun out of trouble.'

'I didn't know you were huggin' an' kissin'.'

'We're not. But Doc's showed me he deserves a square deal. If I stay, he stays.'

'Well—hell,' Morgan gruffed, 'if you say so, that settles it.'

Wyatt said, 'Let's get down to cases. First thing, as I see it, we've got to let the Clantons

138

know this town is closed to them, and we've got to keep it that way. Then we've got to get the run of the county.' He regarded them thoughtfully. 'I'll get a letter off to a feller that can mebbe iron that out for us. Now let's have a look at that map.'

Virgil spread out a map on the table and they all got up to peer over his shoulder.

*   *   *

The next morning Wyatt, stepping into the *Epitaph* office, found J. P. Clum, owner and publisher, back of his desk thumbing through a stack of freshly printed quarter cards.

'Mornin',' Wyatt said, and introduced himself. 'I'm here,' he added, 'to see what we can do about this matter of Ike Clanton.'

Clum scrutinized him sharply. Presently he nodded and handed Wyatt one of the cards. 'That ink's a little wet, but I would think this might bring him right out into the open.'

Wyatt read it and grunted. 'It ought to make him squirm.'

'Mr. Earp,' Clum said, 'I'd like you to know how glad this town is we've got a man of your caliber interested in our problems. You may count on the full support of my paper. I know twenty men you can make special deputies. I can get fifty more if it turns out you need them.'

'That's a nice thing to know. I certainly

couldn't do much without some public support.'

'We're with you. We're right behind you. If you believe we need vigilantes—'

'I'd like to do this legally.' Pointing to the cards, he said, 'Like this.'

*   *   *

Cotton Wilson was reared back in a chair trying to stir up a breeze with his hat when Wyatt stepped into the Marshal's Office. He had a stack of Clum's cards tucked under his arm. Nodding at Cotton he placed these face down on the desk.

'I've been rather expecting you to drop in, Cotton. You're looking fine—real prosperous. Understand you've done a first-rate job looking after the interests of the outlaws hereabouts.'

Cotton grinned somewhat edgily. 'I ain't complainin' none. This here's the best-payin' job I ever latched onto.'

'I can well believe that.' Wyatt was hard put to treat the man with even a show of courtesy. 'I don't suppose,' he said, 'you dropped by to shoot the breeze. Now that you've laid down your character, Cotton, maybe you'd like to turn your cards up and say straight out what errand you're on.'

Wilson said unabashedly, 'Ike wants to make you a deal.'

'What kind of deal?'

'Well, he's got all these cattle pilin' up on him. If you'll give him the nod so's he can ship out of Tombstone, you an' him'll git along powerful easy.' He grinned at Wyatt boldly. 'There might even be a few bucks in it fer you.'

'That's very generous of Ike.'

'We think so. Then I kin tell him it's a deal?'

'I didn't say that.'

The sheriff, frowning, eyed him more carefully. 'Don't be a goddam fool all your life! Lemme draw you a picture. Some day, mebbe, when you're so stove up you can't hardly put one foot ahead of the other, they'll stake you out on a pension of prob'ly twenty stinkin' dollars a month—an' I'm talkin' about if you live that long. Say what you want, Ike's a good guy to work for. I've got me a ranch now an' twenty-five thousand tucked away in the bank. It don't bother my sleep a particle.'

Wyatt said coldly, 'It might bother mine, though.'

'Seems about time you got offa that pulpit. Ellsworth, Wichita, Dodge—Jesus Christ! What's it got you but a assload of misery? A woman who—'

'I think you better get out of here, Cotton.'

'Be smart for once in your life. Clanton's big. Too big fer you to monkey with. He's got friends—even a Congressman. Owns two judges an' every piss-ant lawman in three counties except you Earps. He's got a million dollars

141

worth of steers on his place an' he's sure as hell goin' to move 'em.'

Leaning close, with his breath closing round Wyatt like a fog, he growled, 'Your cut adds up to fifty thousand—cash.'

'Golly. Hard to believe I could be worth so much.'

'You ain't. Like I said, Ike's a good man to tie to.'

'So's the devil, if you don't mind getting singed in the process.'

'Ha ha!' Wilson laughed, and then his eyes winnowed down. 'Fifty thousand's a heap better than a hole in the ground. You think about that.'

'Tell me,' Wyatt said. 'How would you feel about me running for county sheriff?'

Wilson's lips skinned back. 'That ain't scarin' me.'

'I guess everybody sees things different.' Wyatt picked up one of the cards from the face-down stack and pushed it over to the sheriff. 'Here's a little souvenir you can tote back to your boss.'

Wilson turned it over. FIREARMS FORBIDDEN IN THE CITY LIMITS OF TOMBSTONE.

The skin of Wilson's cheeks pulled tight. He said on an outrush of anger, 'Think you can make that stick?'

'I guess we'll pretty soon find out.'

Wilson lost no time getting out to the Clanton ranch. He found Ike Clanton tipped back in a chair against the front of the house catching himself a little shuteye in the shade of a down-down hat. He pushed the felt off his face when he heard the approaching horse. Wilson swung down without opening his mouth, walked up to Ike and dropped the card in his lap. Ike read it casually, tore it up and got out of his chair. 'That his answer?'

'He figures to pull the town from under you, Ike.'

The sheriff followed Clanton into the house. Finn and Billy Clanton, Ike's brothers, were at the kitchen table, eating. Their mother, tired and worn and half sick from work, was scrubbing out a blackened skillet over a tub of greasy water. 'Earp's barrin' guns in Tombstone,' Ike said.

Finn looked up, scowling. Considerable older and meaner than Billy, he shoved back from the table, wickedly cursing.

'Ain't but one thing to do, Finn,' Ike told them. 'Round up Wes Fuller, Ringo, Claibourne an' the McLowry brothers. Tell them I want 'em heeled to the teeth. Tonight we'll ride in an' put this business to the test.'

'Hey, Ike!' young Billy cried. 'How about me?'

'If you're growed enough, you're old

143

enough. Come along if you want.'

Mrs. Clanton stepped away from the tub. 'You can go and get Finn and yourself shot to dollrags, but you leave Billy out of this! He's only a boy.'

'He looks big enough to me. You had me workin' my tail off when I was his age.'

'You ain't gettin' that boy killed.'

'Don't worry about me, Maw. I kin outshoot them Earps left-handed.'

'Get aboard your horse an' get whackin', Finn,' Ike Clanton said, looking hard at the old woman. 'If the kid wants to come along with us you're not stoppin' him.'

*   *   *

A placard on the Fremont Street front of Scheiffelin's Hall announced: EDDIE FOY & COMPANY—IN PERSON—TONIGHT.

Wyatt, near the entrance, stood unarmed in front of this poster checking over the miners and other patrons standing in line as they filed past. There was a deal of racket coming out of the place. A roar of applause shook the windows and the voice of Eddie himself, as the din somewhat abated, could be heard greeting the vociferous crowd. Wyatt, turning out of the line one fellow wearing a pistol, said, 'Sorry, pardner. You'll have to take that gun to the Marshal's Office.'

'Since when?'

'Since right now. There's placards all over. New city ruling.'

'I don't go noplace without my gun.'

'You better take it right out of town then.'

'You Wyatt Earp?'

'That's right.'

'Well—hell. If I got to, I got to.'

Farther down the street, behind the picket fence fronting the O. K. Corral, Ike, Finn and Billy Clanton, Wes Fuller, Billy Claibourne and Tom and Frank McLowry were getting off their horses with a clinking of spur chains. John Ringo, coming out of the shadows, walked up to them. 'He's at Scheiffelin Hall— no gun.'

Ike grinned. 'Let's go.'

*   *   *

Wyatt's back looked broad against the light as he stood in the doorway peering into the semi-darkened hall, listening to the singing.

'Earp!' a voice said sharply.

Wyatt casually turned, holding his hands well out from his body to signify his peaceful intentions. His glance took in the shapes of eight waiting men. Eddie Foy sang on, but around Wyatt now was a creeping stillness. It was plain by their faces they were here for a purpose which had nothing to do with the performance going on inside.

'Been a long time, Ike,' Wyatt said, smiling

145

easily. 'Hello, Ringo. Still renting your gun to the highest bidder?'

Ike started for the doorway. Wyatt stepped into his path. They stood face to face, Clanton burly and scowling, Wyatt coldly watchful. 'Where do you figure you're going?' he asked.

'We come to take in the show. You got any objections?'

'Not if you figure to check those pistols.'

'What *is* this!' Ike Clanton's powerful shoulders tipped forward as he bent at the knees to drive a hand beltward. Before his spread fingers got hold of the weapon, Wyatt's right fist crashed into the big rancher's jaw. In the same split second, his left snatched the pistol from Clanton's holster. Ike staggered back, cursing. His friends were about to make a play for their own guns when Virgil Earp said back of them:

'Hold it!'

Ike, twisting a look blackly over his shoulder, saw Virgil, Morgan, young Jimmy, Clum and Doc Holliday in the middle of the street with leveled shotguns.

'I guess you know most of my brothers,' Wyatt said. 'That jasper in the middle is Doc Holliday, and the gent on his right is Mr. J. P. Clum, esteemed editor of the local paper and presently head of the Tombstone Citizens' Committee.'

Ike made a loud noise. 'That bunch of old grannies are a laugh. If you're smart, you'll haul freight. You're a marked man, mister.'

'You're the one who's marked, Ike. You'd better put on some specs and take a good look at yourself before they start shoveling dirt in on you. This town is fed up with you and that bunch of plug-uglies you run with. There's a new deal in Tombstone. The next time you ride in leave your guns at home or you'll go out feet first.'

He gave Clum the nod, and the group around the publisher closed in on the Clanton hardcases and started moving them off toward the edge of town. Wyatt stood fast, and as they tramped sullenly past, he reached out, catching young Billy Clanton by the arm.

'Just a minute,' he said, pulling the boy off to one side. 'Aren't you a little bit young to be packing a sixshooter?'

'You wanta try me?'

'I would like to prevent you from getting yourself killed. I think you're the one who likes to fancy himself another Billy the Kid, isn't that right? Well, let me tell you something, son. The real Kid's dead, and that's where you'll be if you don't snap out of the way you're heading. How old are you—sixteen?'

'I kin take care of myself,' Billy scowled.

'You'll never make seventeen hanging onto that attitude. You go on home and think it over.'

Billy, starting to turn, went for his pistol. Wyatt kicked it out of his hand. 'Your brothers

147

teach you to draw on an unarmed man?'

Billy, bunching his fists, wading in, started swinging. Wyatt spun him around, roughly shoved him away. Then, picking up the pistol, he tossed it to the boy. 'You don't have to prove anything to me,' he said gruffly. 'Go on home before you get into trouble.'

Startled, bewildered, in a maze of indecision, young Clanton turned and went scuffling off.

*   *   *

Next day, Wyatt, tilted back in a chair on the porch of the Marshal's Office, watched the stage pull in with his brothers, Morgan and Virgil. They watched John Ringo weave up to the coach, pull open a door and haul a laughing Kate Fisher out into his arms, kissing her loudly, then spinning her around to slap a hand against her bustle-covered bottom.

'And there comes trouble,' Wyatt said, softly swearing.

Morgan peered at the woman. 'Who is she?'

'Kate Fisher. Doc's bed partner in Dodge. Damn her mixed-up soul—she just couldn't stay away.'

Virgil said, '*The* Kate Fisher?'

'I said so, didn't I?' Wyatt watched her and the gunfighter cross the street arm in arm. 'Virg, find out where she's stayin'. I better get hold of Doc.'

148

In the Alhambra Saloon, Doc and five others were engaged in draw poker, Doc being currently elbow deep in chips.

One of his companions said, 'Two pair. Aces over.'

'Three small deuces.' Doc grinned and raked in the pot.

As it happened, he looked up just as Kate and Ringo came into the place, still loudly talking. Ringo steered them, without noticing Doc, over to a table right next to him. Apparently Kate had not discovered Doc either.

Doc, though endeavoring to ignore them, was plainly uncomfortable.

Ringo yelled, 'Hey, waiter! Whisky down here—an' leave the bottle.'

'Wake up, Doc. Your deal.'

Doc flipped in his ante, dexterously shuffled and offered the cut. 'Three-card draw, jacks or better.'

'Nice town, huh, Kate?' Ringo said loudly.

Kate, more guardedly, 'You're going to take care of what I wrote you about?'

Ringo laughed. 'Didn't I say so?'

The muscles stood out in Doc's cheeks like white worms. The player across from him said, 'Beats me.' The one on his left said, 'I'll open.'

At the table back of Doc a bottle thumped

against wood. The eyes in Kate's twisting head incredibly widened. She came around in her chair, shaken but glaring. 'Well, well,' she said hoarsely, 'if it ain't the little deputy!'

'I pass,' Doc said, and put down his cards. He sat there, waxen, his knuckles white against the table.

Kate leaned over him. 'Can't you say hello to a flame that's fallen into sparks among the ashes?'

'Cards?' Doc said.

The man next on his left said, 'Three,' and dropped his discard.

The fellow next around, face twitching with fright, desperately managed to whisper: 'One.'

'Say, deputy!' Kate's voice carried over the room. 'Mr. Virtue still keeping you under his wing?'

The whole saloon sat frozen. Doc put down the deck, the sound of it loud as a face being slapped in that brittle quiet. He stood up without haste and got into his coat.

Kate cried shrilly, 'Not leavin' are you, deputy?'

'Sure he's leavin',' Ringo sneered. 'He's fixin' to run over and get his pal.'

'You're drunk,' Doc sighed, looking full at him then.

'Ain't that the way you made your rep— shootin' down drunks?'

'I'm warning you,' Doc said thickly.

'Hear that, folks? Killer Holliday is warnin'

150

me! What am I supposed to do now—drop dead?'

Doc said harshly, 'You're a fool for letting her get you steamed up.'

'An' I say you're yeller!'

'Good night, Ringo.' Doc picked up his hat.

'Oh, no you don't. You ain't skinnin' out till I git done talkin'. I got somethin' to settle with you from Dodge City. I'm goin' over to the hotel and get my persuader.' Ringo stepped up to him, sneering, and tapped his chest. 'I'll be standin' outside, waitin' for you, in about two minutes. You hear? Two minutes!'

Ringo walked around him and pushed through the doors.

The room was a sea of white faces, but none so livid as the face of Doc Holliday, so humiliated and furious it looked as though he would strangle.

'I said I'd see you dead,' Kate whispered.

Wheeling, brushing past the spectacular bosom which seemed in imminent prospect of bursting in all its surging magnificence from the downy nest Kate's skill had fashioned, the consumptive dandy, shrugging out of his coat, walked the length of the bar and went still-faced around it to reappear in the harness of fastened straps that held a shoulder gun in place. A lane opened up before the push of that stare down which Doc, traveling as though to a gallows, slowly made his trek to the doors.

When he appeared on the planks, weirdly

151

illumined in the wavering leap of the orange flares, Ringo, coming off the steps of the Dodge House verandah, moved inexorably into the forty feet of open road which was all that lay between them now.

Ringo's whisker-stubbled lips were pulled apart in a snarl. Doc looked colder than the proverbial well chain. The two shapes paced into pointblank range and were that way, crouching, when a gun blast ripped the groan of silence and scared the quivering bejazus out of half the avid watchers. Both men whipped about as though jerked by a single string.

Ringo's wide-sprung eyes looked frantic. Doc's gray stare was hotly furious.

Virgil Earp, cutting out of the streetside shadows with a shotgun gripped in his white-knuckled fists, called: 'Go for your guns and I'll cut you in half!'

Ringo, reckless with the whisky inside him, tipped back his head in a derisive guffaw. 'Sure—sure,' he chortled, flapping his arms. 'I wouldn't hurt that little bastard fer nothin'.' Doubled up with his guffaws he staggered around in a circle holding onto his sides.

Doc, bitter as gall, stalked off down the street with a towering indignation in the direction of the Cosmopolitan. Virgil, pounding up behind him, got hold of an arm and swung him about just as he reached the hotel door. He was white with an outrage that matched Doc's own.

'What kind of a sucker play was that! That would have been all the excuse Ike Clanton's hunting to start a goddam war around here!'

'What the hell do you think I'm made of?'

'We'll bust those owlhootin' sons of bitches,' Virg said, 'but we'll by God do it our way!'

'You keep on playing patty-cake they'll cut you to pieces!'

Virgil began shaking Doc in a temper. 'You stay out of this!'

'Get your hands off me!'

Virgil slammed him against the door. Doc's pistol jumped into his hand quick as the flick of a lizard's tongue. Shaking with rage, he snarled into Virg's face, 'You better thank God you're Wyatt Earp's brother.' Knocking the marshal's hand away, he spun on his heel and jerked open the door.

'Wait a minute!'

Doc went still in his tracks but he didn't turn. Virgil said back of him, 'If you care anything about Wyatt you'll get out of this town. Having a killer like you on our backs is makin' this job about three times as tough.'

CHAPTER ELEVEN

Wyatt found Doc sitting in his room with a bottle. Doc looked ugly as a teased snake. Wyatt sat down on the bed with a sigh. 'Doc—I understand you're about to pull out of here.'

'You bet your goddam boots I am! I'm taking the stage out of here in the morning!'

'Kind of figured this climate agreed with you. Didn't you tell me you thought it would be good for that cough'?'

'I'll tell you something—I've taken enough!' He got onto his feet and stomped round the room. 'Being here is causing me one hell of a pile of embarrassment. Why, some of these halfwits even think I'm a lawman!'

'Well,' Wyatt said thoughtfully, 'I can't really blame you for cuttin' your string. If things had been different—but this isn't your fight.'

'It sure as hell isn't!' Doc glowered at him, pacing, chewed his lip and came back. He said, more reasonably, 'I could get along in this town if . . . Well, there's no use pushing it at somebody else. What's done is done and no one but a fool would waste time looking back.' He said, watching Wyatt's face, 'I *would* kind of like to square with Ringo though. That sonofabitch really gets in my hair.'

'Don't worry about him. He'll be taken care of along with the Clantons.' Wyatt stood up. 'One thing: I don't want you shovin' out on my account.'

'*Your* account! Are you loco? You got nothing to do with my leaving.'

They looked at each other through several moments of silence. Wyatt said abruptly, 'Well,

154

take care of yourself,' and reached for the door.

'Too bad,' Doc said, 'we can't be in at the finish together. I feel like I'm leaving the best part of me here.' His eyes tightened up; he cleared his throat noisily.

'It's just not in the cards,' Wyatt said. He paused as though he might say something more, maybe making it some harder for Doc to haul his freight. But, shutting his mouth, he turned and went out.

Doc stood there, listening to him go down the stairs. Then, gritting his teeth, he smashed the fist of one hand angrily into the other.

*   *   *

Virgil, the next morning, was in the office reading a batch of mail he had just fetched back from the postal premises, when Wyatt with Clum stepped in off the porch. Virg tossed a folded paper at Clum. 'Here's the answer to that letter Wyatt wrote.'

Wyatt, reading over Clum's shoulder, said, 'That's it! You'll get all the action you're wanting now. How long will it take to round up those fifty deputies you promised?

'Not long,' the newspaperman said grimly. 'I can probably produce them inside of three days.'

'All right, get busy. And try to keep this as quiet as you can.'

155

'Right!' Clum said and, squaring his shoulders, departed like a sergeant who'd been stepped up two full grades.

Several minutes later Morgan and James came in packing a passed-out Billy Clanton between them. Virgil, frowning, said, 'Where'd you pick up that?'

'Alhambra,' Jimmy grinned. 'He was stretched out in the sawdust taking up room for three at the bar.'

'He's got a snootful,' Morg said contemptuously.

'Expect we'd better throw him in and let him sleep it off?'

'Hold on,' Wyatt said. 'Let me think about this.' He tapped the letter they'd discussed with Clum. 'Let me have him.'

Stooping, he flipped young Billy over his shoulder like a sack of oats. 'Think I'll take a little ride out toward Charleston.'

'You droppin' in on the Clantons?' Virgil asked sharply.

'Just a neighborly visit.'

'You crazy?' Morgan growled.

Wyatt carried Billy through the door. On the porch steps he smiled. 'I don't think so.'

'You better take your gun,' Virgil grumbled.

They had fetched Billy's horse. Wyatt untied it and his own from the rail and, laying Billy over the saddle, he took the reins of the Clanton horse, climbed aboard his own and said, 'Pass him up to me.' He waved the letter at them. 'This is all the ammunition I'll need.' He gathered up the reins of both mounts. 'If I'm not back in a couple or three hours you can have John Clum and his Citizens' Committee come drag me out of there,' he said with a laugh.

*   *   *

Wyatt, still riding the cruppers behind his saddle and with the prostrate Billy draped unconsciously across it, jogged along through the bright slant of morning sunlight as apparently unconcerned as though this were something he did every day of the week. The whole country figured the Clanton tribe to be rougher than cobs and Wyatt reckoned they probably were, but when he came up with a hunch to do a certain thing he pretty generally did it, come hell or highwater. There was some good in this kid if a man had the patience to dig it out.

He kept his eyes skinned, not being minded to ride into an ambush, but about all he saw on the ride out was cattle. There seemed, giving credence to the stories he'd heard, to be thousands of head tramping over this range, a whole heap too many for the grass that was on it. Ike could mighty soon be in a bind unless he moved them; and there was another angle that would be gnawing at Ike. The most of these critters were almost certainly stolen stock—

157

though a man might find proving this difficult. These were longhorns, wild but good rustlers. Trouble was, there wasn't much left on this range, including cactus.

After a time Wyatt picked out the buildings of the Clanton headquarters. These were sun-warped and paintless, appearing sadly neglected. Most of the windows were shutterless; several of them did not even have any glass. A board above the twelve-foot top of the horse gate bore a single word: CLANTON. Below, attached to the two center rails with baling wire was another reading bluntly: TRESPASSERS WILL BE SHOT ON SIGHT.

Wyatt put his horse through the gate, hauled Billy's horse after him, and pushed the rickety affair shut, dropping a wire loop over the end pole. He rode on toward the house. There were a few parched geraniums in a circle of stones a few feet from the pump.

Wyatt, getting down, hauled Billy off and vigorously shook him. He looked about as sick as the geraniums, but he was conscious. Wyatt shook him again, finally slapped his face when the lad showed signs of buckling at the knees. 'Stand on your feet, boy.'

Billy shook his head and peered around like a halfwit. Mrs. Clanton came out, gnarled hands half hidden in a twist of her skirt.

'Afternoon, ma'am.' Wyatt touched his hat. 'Sorry to be the bearer of unpleasant news, but Billy here got himself liquored up.'

158

'I don't know what in the world's to become of that boy. I can't think what I'm goin' to do with him.'

'I'll get him sobered up.'

The old lady, distraught and obviously in a flutter, led the way into the house which, though scrupulously clean, was frowsy as to furnishings. Wyatt propelled Billy by the scruff of the neck. Turned loose, Billy slumped into a chair he pulled out from the table, sheepishly avoiding his mother's eye. She fetched them both steaming mugs of coffee. 'The way he's goin',' Mrs. Clanton said, 'he'll end up like his father, shot down stealing cattle. Ike and Finn are well along the road.'

She scooted a worried glance at the marshal. 'I can't stop them. I've preached till I'm hoarse. It's too late for them but why in the name of God—'

Wyatt nodded. 'Think you're pretty tough, son? I've never seen a gunslinger yet that lived to celebrate his thirty-fifth birthday.'

He stood up. 'I thank you for the coffee, ma'am.'

'Mr. Earp,' Billy stammered, 'I—nothin', nothin'—never mind.'

'Think I don't know what's inside of you? I had two older brothers. They fought in the War. I was too young. But, by gollies, I sure done my best to live up to them—just the same as you're tryin' to live up to Ike an' Finn.'

'You—you really know about that, huh?'

159

'It's a natural thing. But I've learned one thing about gunfighters. No matter how good you are there's generally somebody just a shade faster, and the more you work with a gun the quicker you're goin' to meet that man.'

It was plain enough that Wyatt was reaching the boy. Billy was turning over Wyatt's words, frowning, wary but confused, not knowing what to think. Wyatt sat down again, close to the boy, waving Mrs. Clanton back.

'It ain't,' Billy said, 'that I want to be a gunfighter. It's—it's—just that sometimes I—I get so goddam lonesome.'

'Gunfighting, boy, is a pretty lonesome trade. Matter of fact, I get lonely myself.'

'You? Aw—you mean that?' The marshal's words appeared to have a considerable impact on the boy.

'Gunfighters are the loneliest men on the face of God's earth, Billy. They live in fear, generally die without a dime—or a woman. Without even a friend.'

'I—I never thought about it that way. I always figured—gosh! You ain't pullin' my leg are you, Mr. Earp?'

'I surely ain't, Mr. Clanton.' Wyatt chuckled. 'My friends all call me, Wyatt, Billy.'

Billy's eyes were round, but something was troubling him. He said in a voice that was wistful, uncertain, 'I always kind of had a cravin' to be—'

'To be what, Billy?'

160

'You ain't goin' to laugh, are you?'

'I won't laugh.'

'Well—I'd sure would like to be a vetinery. You know, one of them docs that takes care of animals. I like to be around dogs an' horses. Seems like I got a way with them, only—only Ike an' Finn, they claim that's sissy stuff. Is it?'

'I don't think so. Wanting to be a vet is a right fine thing. Seems to me like it is.' He got up again. Billy grabbed at his sleeve.

'Could I come talk to you sometime about it? I mean—'

'Come anytime, son. Maybe we can work it so's you can go to one of them veterinarian schools.'

Mrs. Clanton came forward. 'You listen to the marshal. Never mind what your brothers say—you listen to the marshal. He's a man whose word don't need no bond. When he says a thing's so, it's so forever.'

The boy put his arms around his mother, hiding his face behind her head. 'I won't do it no more, Maw. I swear I won't. I'll die in bed, like you wanted Paw to, with my boots off.'

'Oh, son!' she cried. 'Son . . .'

Wyatt walked softly out of the house.

He was about to mount up when the sound of hoofs coming fast pulled him round. Ike and Cotton Wilson in a fog of dust came tearing down the lane from the gate. Ike Clanton came off his horse in one jump. His face was wild. 'What you doin' here?'

161

'I brought your kid brother home, drunk.'
Wyatt tried to step past Ike to get on his horse,
but Clanton grabbed his arm. Wyatt yanked
the arm free. Ike's other fist slid down to his
gun.

'You're leavin', all right, but not on no
horse. Start hikin'.'

'That would be a mistake that might get you
killed. Some of my friends in Tombstone are
apt to get the wind up if I'm not back soon.'

'That don't cut no ice with me! You're outa
your bailiwick—'

'You sure about that?' Wyatt, grinning
thinly, took a paper out of his pocket. 'I expect
it'll be a disappointment to you, but this is my
appointment as a United States Marshal.
Here, look it over.'

Ike stood there stunned. The sheriff's jaw
sagged.

Clanton came out of his confusion first. He
backed off a step, cuffed some dust off his
pantslegs and rasped the hand across his jowls.
'Wait a minute,' he growled. 'Let's talk about
this. I know we ain't often seen eye to eye, but
I got nothin' ag'in you, personal. I ain't lookin'
for no fight, but goddam it you got to stop
crowdin' me. Why—' he said gruffly, 'why
don't we set a spell an' hash over this thing?
I'll make you the best deal I know how. The
best damn deal any star packer ever got
dumped in his lap.'

'The only deal,' Wyatt said, 'I'll ever make

162

with you would be to run that herd straight back into Mexico.' Shoving past the two frustrated, angry men, he got into his saddle and rode off up the lane. He should have been a little nervous; he had every right to be. If he had turned for one backward look his would have seen Clanton struggling to throw off the clamped grip with which Cotton Wilson was desperately combatting every attempt the burly rancher made to bring his gun into line with the marshal's back.

*   *   *

When the new U. S. Marshal returned to the county seat, a reception committee composed of his brothers and J. P. Clum were anxiously standing before the door of the town Marshal's Office. Wyatt, pulling up before the hitch-rail, eyed them quizzically. 'Where's the funeral?'

'By God, you had us worried,' Virgil declared, letting out his breath:

'What happened out there?' Morgan asked.

Wyatt swung down, tossed his reins over the rail, ducked under it himself and stepped up onto the porch. 'Better get your men in, John,' he said to Clum. 'It looks like we got a war on our hands.'

He entered the office, the rest of them following.

*   *   *

Back at the Clanton ranch Ike was furiously pacing the kitchen. Standing around the room were Ringo, Finn Clanton and Tom and Frank McLowry. In the background Kate Fisher, hovering over the stove, was brewing up a fresh pot of coffee. Neither Billy nor his mother were present at this conclave.

'What's keepin' that coffee?' Ringo growled.

'Be ready in a minute.'

Cotton Wilson came in, mopping his face and puffing.

Ike jabbed at him with an angry finger. 'You see the judge?'

Cotton jerked his head. 'I seen him.'

'Well, what the hell did he have to say?'

'No help there. Claims there ain't no legal way he kin keep a U. S. Marshal outa the county. He was packin' up to leave. Prob'ly more'n halfway to Utah by now. That town's really got the wind up. You never seen so many scairt fools in your life.'

Ike slammed the table with a furious fist. Frank McLowry said nervous-like, 'Mebbe it's time we was all pack in' up.' And Cotton Wilson grumbled, 'It sure don't look good—don't look good at all, Ike. Before you know it that bunch will hev a whole army of gun throwers. They're swearin' in deputy U. S. Marshals fast as they kin write their names. You can't sell the herd an' you can't git a shippin' point.'

'Ain't you the little ray of sunshine!' This from Kate, handing out mugs of coffee. 'Why don't you dig a hole and crawl into it?'

Cotton glared.

Finn Clanton said, 'Won't make no deal, eh?'

'Only deals bein' made is fer us to git planted.'

'Shut up!' Ike roared, and took a turn around the room. 'One thing we can do, by God. We didn't have no trouble before them Earps took over this country. Get rid of them Earps an' the rest of that crowd'll cave like a bunch of pukin' pigeons!'

Tom McLowry said, 'Mebbe we wouldn't hev to go that far. It's Wyatt thet's holdin' thet whole bunch t' taw. Git rid of him—'

'We'll get rid of all of 'em,' Ike snarled, banging his fists on the table.

'Makes sense to me,' Ringo drunkenly offered. 'Git rid of them Earps an' we can take over everythin'.' He twisted his head to send a wink at Kate. 'I'll take care of Doc Holliday myse'f.'

'We'll ambush the bunch of them,' Ike said.

'Shoot 'em into dollrags,' Finn Clanton laughed. 'Cut off their heads an' put 'em up on poles. That'll show'em!'

The sheriff said, 'It's Wyatt an' that sneerin' sonofabitchin' Doc—'

'They've broke up,' Kate said. 'Doc's pulling

165

out. Ringo made him look like a monkey. It did my poor heart good to see him crawl.'

'You talkin' about *Doc*?' Finn looked at her skeptically, and Frank McLowry said, 'That's a powerful lot to swaller, even if you seen it.'

'Never mind,' Ike growled. 'We'll get them all.'

'What about Clum an' his Citizens' Committee?' the sheriff said. 'What about them deputies Wyatt's swearin' in?'

'Cut off the head and the snake may wriggle but it sure as hell won't be doin' no bitin',' Finn said. 'Them boys got a lot of family pride. Comes right down to the pinch—'

'Comes down to the pinch,' Ike grinned, 'they'll be standin' alone. Let's quit the yappin' an' get down to brass tacks.'

He saw the sheriff sleeving off his face again. 'You scared of this, Cotton?'

'Well, Christ, I can't shoot another lawman.' He swallowed uncomfortably. 'I—I can't do you no good in a deal like that.'

'You're in this up to your goddam neck! You're stayin' in—savvy?'

The sheriff's eyes squirmed away and John Ringo's drunken laugh filled the room.

Ike finished his coffee. 'We'll fix it up to get Wyatt when they make their last rounds. Tonight, I'm talkin' about.'

'You better get all of them,' Kate said vindictively.

'We'll get 'em,' Ike said.

166

CHAPTER TWELVE

It may stagger the contemporary reader to envisage a group homicide as coldbloodedly conceived and entered upon as the bushwhacking planned for the Earps by the Clantons. But these people were feudists; with them a grudge was a killing affair and Ike had never gotten over the gnawing suspicion that his father's death had been engineered by an Earp. And a lot of side issues were wrapped up in his decision. He was tied in with Curly Bill, self-styled leader of the local 'cow boys', a confederacy of outlaws numbering over four hundred hard-riding men, and Ike was pretty certain the Earps knew this. Pima County in those days was the wildest place in the American West, if not the wildest place the West has ever known And Ike had told the whole truth when he said, 'Get rid of them Earps an' the rest of that crowd'll cave like a bunch of pukin' pigeons!' Get rid of the Earps and they could plunder at will.

*   *   *

Back in town that night it was getting along toward midnight when young Jimmy Earp came into the office with a jug of hot coffee. Wyatt, half across the desk with his face in his

167

arms, looked up, fully roused, when the door swung open. Seeing his brother he sat up, stretched his arms to get the kinks from his back, and knuckled his eyes, managing a grin when he smelled the hot java.

'Tired?' Jimmy asked.

'Yeah. Guess I must have been dozing. How's things outside, steaming up like usual?'

'Nothing new. Betty thought you might like something hot.'

Jimmy poured the smoking liquid into a tin cup. Wyatt drank it and smacked his lips, afterward wiping the wet ends of his mustache. 'Hits the spot, all right. Whew!'

Young Jimmy, at the window, was staring out at the town. 'Seems powerful quiet—too quiet, Virg thinks. You reckon we'll have to fight it out with that bunch?'

'Wish I knew,' Wyatt said reflectively. 'Ike's in a bind. Those stolen cows have gobbled up all his graze. One way or another he's sure got to move 'em. He *might* just decide this deal is too rough and push them back into Mexico, but that wouldn't be like him. The McLowrys are in this, too—probably some more of that Curly Bill bunch. This no-gun edict has hit them all. They daren't come in here without their guns . . . When you look the facts of this straight in the face, they'd be ridin' high except for us Earps.'

He got up and stomped about. 'There's another angle, too. There's a lot of counts

168

piled up against Ike. He's managed to get rid of most of the witnesses and he's likely wondering why I didn't fetch him in today. Time's runnin' out on him and don't think he doesn't know it.'

Jimmy, slouched with a hip on a corner of the desk, looked as though his mind was miles and miles away. Wyatt, grinning, said, 'Itchin' to get back to Californy?'

'I been thinkin' about it.'

'Must be quite a girl.'

'You ought to see her,' Jimmy cried enthusiastically. 'But I'm glad I came over here. It's the first time we've really been away from each other in the two years I've known her. It's made me see things clearer. It's like I'm all unstuck, only half a person. I'm glad I found this out before I—' He looked around at his brother guiltily. 'I'm sorry, Wyatt.'

'Hell, don't mind me. I'm glad you found out, too, Jimmy. Best thing you can do is go back there and marry her. Leave star packin' to the fools like me.' He picked up his hat. 'Guess I better be makin' the rounds.'

Jimmy said contritely, 'Why don't you go in the back an' stretch out? I'll make the check. You look beat.'

'Guess I could use a nap,' Wyatt said through a yawn.

'Go ahead,' the youngster urged. 'I'll wake you up when I get back.'

'You're a good kid, Jimmy. Did I ever tell

169

you that?'

The boy, grinning self-consciously, strapped on a shell belt and stepped out on the street.

*   *   *

From the mouth of the O. K. Corral not too much of Fremont Street was in sight. The livery business was on the south side of the wide dirt road and the business establishments in this block were not of the character which sought night trade; only the O. K. Corral did a round-the-clock schedule.

It was crowding midnight when James Earp, moving along the north side checking doors, came past the dark front of the *Epitaph* office. The town's main drag was Allen Street one block south. There were congregated the better hotels, saloons and eating places, a good portion of the night life so frequently making the public prints.

The one hotel on Fremont, the Aztec House, was one block west. Jimmy could see its feeble lights but these did nothing to dispel the roundabout blackness of deep-piled shadows. He didn't mind the dark; it was an old story with him and an adjunct he'd expected. But he didn't much care for the quality of the quiet that seemed to grow more solid, more uncannily stealthy, the nearer he came to the O. K. Corral. There were no bird or cricket sounds, only this vacuum of soundless hush through which his bootsteps echoed hollowly. He could be heard even though he could not be seen well enough to be distinguished if there were anyone around.

He scoffed at himself but the tightness building inside him would neither go away nor loosen. He felt the probe of unseen eyes and told himself he was acting like a chicken-livered fool. Just the same, he wished now he had not volunteered to make this round.

He was directly across from the O. K. Corral when a horse whinnied sharply, breaking off in full voice. He thought to hear lesser sounds, perhaps a scuffle, the crack of leather. He crossed the dust of the road, eyes narrowed, catfooted, the gun half lifted in his hand as he tried to pierce the heavy blackness shrouding the livery's entrance.

As he drew nearer, Jimmy thought to pick out a vague blur of movement back where the night loomed inkiest. Stopped cold, he peered wide-eyed, and had about convinced himself it was nothing but a figment of his imagination when flame and the lethal burst from six pistols blasted the silence into a cacophony of tumbling echoes.

Jimmy staggered, was whipped around in the slap of bullets, thrown against the scarred post of a hitching rail, down which he sagged into a motionless heap. His hat, fallen off, careened around in a circle and came to a wobbly stop about a foot away from his limp left hand.

A flurry of hoofbeats, thudding over the street, dimmed out in a diminishing whisper of sound.

*　　　*　　　*

This was October of 1881. Thus far, during his tenure of office as town marshal, Virgil Earp had little more to show for his efforts than his predecessor, Marshal Fred White, whom Curly Bill had shot down in his infamous demonstration of the 'road agent's spin.' Shootings continued unabated and, when nothing else could relieve their boredom, cowhands in from the roundabout ranches blew off excess steam in target matches that, as often as not, wound up in a gunfight. George Parsons, generally preoccupied with affairs of the soul, not long before had recorded in his diary: 'Benson Corral man shot Calhoun but didn't hurt him much. Things continue lively.' Several months back the Alhambra Saloon had been 'treed' and taken over by Curly Bill's gang of roughneck cowboys who had then run everyone off the streets. And now James Earp lay dead in the dust. Lively times indeed!

*　　　*　　　*

Wyatt, sitting bolt upright on his cot in the Marshal's Office, had no idea what had awakened him. But almost at once he heard a dim outburst of shouts. Stamping into his boots he jumped up, flung his gun belt around him and ran onto the street, the racket off yonder easily guiding him to the scene of his brother's murder.

A considerable crowd was standing around. He found Virgil's wife sitting on the ground with Jimmy's head in her lap. Lanterns showed her too stricken for tears. Morgan, kneeling nearby, had hold of one of the youngster's wrists. Virgil, back of Betty, had his hands on her shoulders. Morgan, dropping Jimmy's hand, rose to his feet just as Wyatt shoved through to them. 'He's gone,' Morgan said with his face hard as flint.

'Why,' Virgil whispered, 'did I send for him? Why?'

'You can't take the blame for this on yourself,' Morgan growled. 'It's bound to have been some of those goddam cowboys.'

Wyatt strode off into the corral where he sagged against the rails trying to shut out the sight of his dead brother's body. A hand, reaching out of the shadows, gently squeezed Wyatt's shoulder.

Wyatt, recognizing Doc, said, 'I thought you'd gone.'

'Not yet. Not sure I will now. Things are shaping up pretty fast around here.'

Wyatt rasped his jaw. 'This is plain enough for me. Ike has called the play. Look around at those shells—a typical Clanton stunt by God. Well,' he said, heading back toward the street, 'he ain't goin' to get away with it.'

Going back to the Cosmopolitan, the consumptive dentist-turned-gambler put down half a bottle of his 'cough medicine,' strapped on his gun rig and returned to the street. A few minutes later Kate, in her boarding house, looked up from throwing things into a trunk to see the door burst open and her old wrestling partner, like a volcano about to erupt, standing there baleful as a scorpion with its tail up.

She stood petrified with fright as Doc, stepping into the room, cuffed the door shut behind him. 'Taking a little trip?'

Kate thought her knees were going to come apart right under her. She'd had plenty of chance to know from firsthand experience just how mean a varmint he could be when he put his mind to it.

Watching him the way one snake will another, she commenced to edge away, trying to put the bed between them. Beneath his natty mustache Doc's mouth writhed into a sneer. Step for step he moved inexorably after her, chuckling deep in his throat as her frantic eyes got bigger and brighter, her flaccid cheeks more pinched and chalky.

'No, Doc—no!'

'Start talking.'

'I don't—'

'Never mind the lies. You been layin' with

174

Ringo. He was in on it. Talk or by God I'll twist it out of you.'

She came up against the wall and there was no place else to go. She cringed and shook. Her hands came up as though by so frail a barrier she desperately thought to fend him away. 'I—you got to believe me! I didn't want that boy to get killed—'

'Talk, you slut, before I cut the nose right out of that face.'

'You know how it's been. I've messed everything up—but it's part your fault, too! You know how I am about you. I—I thought if Wyatt was out of the way you'd come back, that things would be like they was before . . . I must have been out of my mind,' she sobbed, but Doc's bleak face did not soften at all.

'Where—when did they hatch up this deal?'

'Today. Out at Ike's ranch.'

'Who was there?'

She tried to hedge. 'What do you want from me, Doc?'

'The names of every whippoorwill out there, every sonofabitch that pulled a trigger!'

'But it—they never knew it was James.'

Doc started to reach and she cried with her eyes rolling back like a bronc's, 'It was Ike and Finn, Cotton Wilson, the McLowrys—'

'Wasn't Ringo there?'

She bobbed her head, speechless, then grabbed hold of new breath and said, 'Wes Fuller, too.'

There was murderous rage in every inch of Doc's face, in the blazing eyes, the bared glint of his teeth.

Kate twisted away and tripped over a stool. A scream of sheer fright came wildly out of her as she scrabbled on hands and knees to get up. 'Don't kill me, Doc—don't kill me!' she moaned.

She sprang up in a terrified lunge for the door but he cut her off and she dived under the bed, crying, 'No! No! No!' She came up on the far side and, hardly knowing what she did, rushed into a corner and found herself trapped. Her eyes bulged in horror as the gambler stalked after her, nastily grinning. Babbling, whimpering, clothes disheveled, cheeks pasty, she looked altogether crazy.

She had plenty of right to with Doc's strangling fingers reaching for her throat. 'Doc! Don't!' she gasped, almost swooning with terror.

She closed her eyes to shut out the look of him and could still see, as against a pink fog, the kaleidoscopic whirl of light and shadow, but the hands never touched her. She heard his racking cough and her jerked-open half crazy eyes saw him reeling and gasping, clutching at his chest as he floundered blindly toward the bed.

Like a terrified rabbit Katie jumped for the door.

But with her hand on the knob she paused

176

for a backward look to find him, still gagging and gasping, groveling on the bed in the frightful doubled-over agony of the continuing paroxysm . . . saw him tangled in the bedspread, writhing off onto the floor.

She had the door open now. Shaking, uncontrollably whimpering, she stumbled into the hallway. But her legs would not take her farther. She stood mired in her own confusion, bound to the man as with ropes of steel. She peered again and was lost. 'Doc! My God—oh, Doc!' she sobbed, and ran back, dropping onto the floor, frenziedly flinging her arms about him.

She got him onto his knees. The coughing stopped. Doc looked at her in wonder, then his glance fell away. He dragged a sleeve across his mouth and swore. Their cheeks came together, his arms locked tight around her. 'Forgive me, Kate,' he whispered into her hair.

She got one of his arms hooked over her shoulder and, someway, got him onto his feet. 'It's goin' to be all right, honey. It will be all right. Put your weight on me. I'm going to take care of you . . .'

*　　　*　　　*

Perhaps a few minutes later, back at the Marshal's Office Wyatt, sighing deeply, snuffed the lamp in the bracket above his desk and, clapping on his hat, stepped out onto the porch and locked the door.

He thrust the key in his pocket, bleakly eyeing the street, the shafts of light and deeper blackness, the three or four hipshot horses half asleep on tied reins in front of the Alhambra and the Occidental next door. Bob Hatch's, just east of the Alhambra, was dark and, as he stared with bitter thoughts, remembering the girl who would be waiting for Jimmy across the empty miles, a sudden stirring in the shadows dropped the spread of his hand to leather. The gun leaped free and he whipped it up.

'Wyatt! Wyatt—over here! It's me, Billy Clanton!'

Wyatt, gun leveled, walked into the pooled gloom of the arcade's overhang. 'What are you doing here, Billy?'

The boy swallowed uncomfortably. 'Ike told me to find you.'

Wyatt pouched his gun. His left fist lashed out, meatily striking the boy in the face. Flung backward by the blow, he caromed off a hitching rail and fell into a water trough.

Gasping, teeth chattering and thoroughly soaked, he fished himself out and stood dripping and silent until Wyatt took hold of the front of his shirt. 'I—I never had nothin' to do with that—with what happened to Jimmy. I never knew—'

Wyatt drew back his fist with a snarl.

'You got to believe me!' Billy wailed. 'You got to!'

178

The bunched shirt gradually slipped from Wyatt's loosening grip. 'I'm sorry, son. I shouldn't of done that. Just because your name is Clanton ... I'm sorry, boy.' The marshal stepped back. 'What was it you wanted to tell me?'

It was hard to make out the boy's face in these shadows.

'Ike—Ike wants to meet with you and your brothers. He wants to meet you man to man, he says, with no interference from Clum or his bunch.'

Wyatt eyed the boy a long moment, wishing there might have been more light on him, or some other manner by which he could better gauge the sincerity of this message. 'Where is Ike now?' he said finally.

'I don't know.'

The marshal snorted. 'Well, you can tell him I'll sure enough meet him. How many's he bringin'?'

'Finn, Ike himself, Ringo and the McLowrys. Six of us.'

'Where's this meetin' to be, and when?'

Billy hitched at his pants and said, 'Sun-up. at the O. K. Corral.'

'It would be there,' Wyatt growled. 'Who did he think he was shootin' tonight?'

'I don't know anything about that. I didn't even hear about it till it was over an' done with.'

'I'll take your word for it. You said six of

179

you. Who's the other one?'

The boy shifted his weight. 'I'll be comin' with them.'

'That all the sense you've got? Don't be a fool! Give yourself a chance, boy.'

Billy said doggedly, 'You can't make a silk purse out of a sow's ear. I've thought about this thing—real hard. But I'm in it. I'm a Clanton, too. How could I stay out of it? Ike an' Finn, they're my brothers, you know. Can't—' He resumed desperately, 'Can't you understand, Mr. Earp? Mebbe it ain't what I want, but they're my *brothers*.'

Wyatt nodded. 'I understand, son.'

For a little longer the boy stood there, watching him. Then, whirling with a catch of breath he could not altogether hide, he disappeared into the deeper dark.

CHAPTER THIRTEEN

Morgan, Wyatt and Virgil, half an hour later, sat grimly about the cleared table in the kitchen of Virgil's house at the western end of Fremont Street. Wyatt had just given the others the news. Betty Earp, one hand on her husband's shoulder, stood rigidly, palely, staring at Wyatt.

'How can you—*all of you*—sit there so calmly, and discuss what amounts to cold-blooded murder! How *can* you?'

'It ain't easy,' Wyatt said, 'but it's sure got to be done.'

And Morgan said, 'Jimmy'll never rest easy until—'

'You make me tired, you men with your antiquated notions of 'honor'—How do *you* know,' she stormed, 'what Jimmy would have wanted? At least,' she said bitterly, 'you can take enough deputies along to make it even!'

Virgil shook his head. 'Now, Sugar, it was just us Ike invited. He ruled out Clum, an' that's just the same as rulin' out deputies. It's us Earps he aims to bust caps at.'

'And has taken good care to make sure he gets the job done. Six to three—you ought to have your heads looked at!'

'Well, it's done now,' Morgan said. 'Wyatt's give his word—'

'To a bunch of bushwhackers who have just cut down his brother!'

Wyatt sighed.

Virgil said, 'Betty, you don't understand. This is personal between us boys an' the Clanton—'

'But they've got the McLowrys and Ringo in on it. You're lawmen, all three of you! You've no business,' she cried, 'to put a personal issue above the safety of this town. Your duty is to the people, not to your stubborn pride.'

When they refused to comment she seemed ready to hit them. 'Oh, you proud, proud

181

men—look at you!' Her scathing eyes raked the three impartially. 'And what about me? And your children?' she lashed at Virgil. 'Have you given us a thought? You're not humans! You're no better than animals!'

Virgil, scowling, got out of his chair. 'That's enough!'

She whirled on Morgan. 'Have you told your wife she'll be a widow tomorrow?'

Virgil roughly took hold of her shoulder. 'I'd think you'd better leave the room.'

She glared through red-rimmed eyes and stalked out. None of the brothers looked at each other. In that frozen silence they resembled effigies of men, plaster facsimiles, colored and clothed, but with no more warmth than you'd find in a bartender's heart.

Betty, cheeks tear-streaked, reappeared in the doorway. 'Virgil—your son wants to kiss you goodnight.'

Virgil, gritting his teeth, stamped out of the room. Morgan and Wyatt swapped uncomfortable glances. 'Could we do it without him?'

'It's rough enough now—two to one—an' Ringo in it. Maybe,' Morgan scowled, 'you ought to of given us a little more leeway. Well, the hell with it. If we're going to cash in our chips, we'll cash 'em, I reckon. I know one thing: I'll take that bastardly Ike along with me!'

Wyatt sighed heavily. He pushed back from

the table, got up and put on his hat. 'See you in the mornin'.'

Morgan nodded, and followed him out.

Wyatt struck off through the dark, prowling aimlessly, morosely preoccupied with the things in his head. Not that he didn't have his guard up. He was always vigilant—it was the price he paid for continued existence—but he didn't in these few moments particularly care what happened to him. He was filled with a great and almighty weariness, a surfeit of gunplay. He would have liked to walk off and put it all behind.

In some ways Betty was right. Ike had tricked him. Trading on a man's pride, his vanity, Ike—in ruling Clum out—had played the three of them for suckers. He had gambled that Wyatt, all steamed up over Timmy, would be too outraged and proud not to fall for this deal. Ike had them where he wanted them now.

Wyatt went down the middle of Fremont Street, walking east through the dust in a kind of numb shuffle. He stopped for some while when he came to the corral, just standing there, staring at it, cursing it finally before he moved on.

At the corner he turned into Fourth Street, passing the dark hulk of the Post Office, continuing south. There were still a couple of dim-lighted windows at the back of the Can-Can Restaurant on the northwest corner of

183

Allen. He considered going in for a steak, but finally plodded on, headed for his room at the Cosmopolitan. Old memories, old faces, tugged at him, taking his mind back to better times, days when he hadn't the woes of the world on his back.

He stepped up onto the porch and pulled open the door. In the dim hallway, still troubled, he paused in front of his door and stood a moment in meditation. Then he put out his hand and took hold of the knob, but he did not at once turn it. He stared over a shoulder at the door across the way. He chewed on his lip and frowning, wheeling, went over, brought up his hand and gave an undecided knock.

'Come in,' Doc growled. 'And if it's trouble you're huntin', come a-shootin'.'

Wyatt pushed open the door.

Doc lay sprawled on the bed, still with his clothes on, one arm, hanging over, almost touching the floor. On the boards, a little way from his fingers, Wyatt saw a tipped-over empty whisky bottle. And he thought how like the skinny bastard this was.

'Oh, it's you,' Doc muttered, bleary-eyed.

Stepping over to the bed Wyatt shook the gambler's shoulder. 'Why the hell don't you go to bed proper? Sit up! I'll help you get out of those clothes. You smell like a calfin' pen!'

'Go away,' Doc mumbled. 'I'm sick. Leave me alone.'

184

'You ought to be sick, swillin' that coffin varnish.' Wyatt shook him again. Doc lay as limp as a bar rag. There appeared to be something folded into his left fist. Out of idle curiosity Wyatt pried open the fingers. He found himself holding a broken watch. Engraved on the back was a minute inscription. *To our Beloved Son, Doctor John Holliday.*

Rolling Doc over onto his back Wyatt caught hold of him by the shoulders, trounced him around and yelled, 'Doc! Wake up! You hear me? Wake up!'

Doc groaned and coughed.

'Damn it,' Wyatt snarled, 'for Chrissake, wake up! You can't let me down now!'

'Take your hands off him,' Kate said, coming out of a horsehair chair in the shadows. Stepping nearer she turned up the wick of the lamp. 'Can't you see he's dying?'

The marshal stared in disbelief. He hands fell open, allowing Doc to drop back on the rumpled bed. Shaking his head, still with that baffled expression on his face, Wyatt backed over to the door and out into the hall.

Inside his own room Wyatt, slamming the door, strode over to a chest of drawers, yanked open the top one, hauled out a bottle and stood impatiently picking and prying at the cork. In mounting exasperation, he broke off the neck of the bottle against the chest and upended it, downing a king-sized slug, nearly

185

half of it trickling off his chin onto his shirtfront. 'Whew!' he sighed on an outgoing breath, and stood there scowling, trying to figure this, trying to gee up Kate's words to the facts as he knew them. It just didn't seem possible old Doc could be actually on the way out. He was still standing there when a quick tap of knuckles spun him round to face the door. He let go of the bottle. His blurring hand came up with a pistol. He went into a crouch as the door cracked open.

His jaw sagged numbly when he found himself peering unbelievingly at Laura. He couldn't seem to collect his wits.

'I was in Tucson.' She considered him gravely. 'Everyone's been talking about you and the Clantons. It's all over the country. Is it true what they're saying?'

Wyatt swallowed uncomfortably. 'What are they saying?'

'That you're going to shoot it out. It—it's just a crazy rumor, isn't it?' She searched his face. Her shoulders appeared to sag a little. 'It's true. You really intend to.'

'But—' He couldn't seem to find the things he had any right to tell her. His face turned bleak. 'They killed Jimmy, Laura— bushwhacked him. Shot him down without a chance.'

The steadiness of her regard turned him restive. He discovered he still held the pistol. He pouched it, embarrassed, and stepped back

186

a little, frowning. The hopelessness that turned him inwardly hollow played on his nerves and stirred up a gnawing feeling of guilt. He lashed out at her angrily, 'Can't you understand this is something I have to do?'

'Yes. I can see that. You will always be confronted with these things you have to do. I don't know why I bothered to come here.' She smiled wanly. 'It was pretty foolish of me, wasn't it?'

Her eyes watched him, still with the faint shine of hope; when that faded, when she would have left, he cried, 'Laura!' and she turned back. He came toward her. 'Laura, I'm scared,' he said.

It was a strange admission for the Lion of Tombstone, the Iron Marshal. As though a dam somewhere inside had burst, he rushed on. 'Someone told me, years ago, that this would happen. I couldn't believe it. I—I can't understand myself. Something's wrong with me. It's like everything inside had suddenly been ripped out of me. That's crazy, ain't it?'

She could only stand there dumbly.

He hauled her to him. His arms closed round her. He clutched her as though he would never let her go. 'I need you, Laura!'

She could feel him shaking. She passed her stroking hands through his hair. 'I've wanted so long, and so much, to hear that.'

'You'll stay. You *will* stay, won't you?'

'Yes. I suppose I could stay—tonight,

anyway, while you need me. But tomorrow . . .'
She closed the lids of her eyes against tears,
'Tomorrow you'll be Wyatt Earp again, the
Stonefaced Marshal, the scourge of bandits.
Tomorrow you'll be embarrassed to remember
you could bring yourself to call for help. You'll
be ashamed of it, Wyatt. Or you'll be dead.'

'Just hold me,' Wyatt said.

She put her arms around him and pressed
his cheek against her breast.

CHAPTER FOURTEEN

The first creeping rays of the awakening sun
touched a far hanging bank of clouds with
pink, and a lot of folks saw this who would not
normally have been up. Except for perhaps
Doc Holliday, the whole town was aware that
today was special—extra special—because
unless one side or the other begged off the
Earps and the Clantons would meet for a
shootout. Through the night this news had
spread like wildfire and already the windows
and doors of establishments overlooking the
prospective site of the battle were crammed
with avid, excited faces. Even the roofs were
alive with people. Betting was rampant.

On the seat of a spring wagon bound for
town Mrs. Clanton sat hunched over the reins
with her mouth tight locked and her eyes like

agate. Ahead, the black rim of the mesa showed a capping of gold as, leaping to her feet, she began to whip up the team.

In Virgil's kitchen Betty Earp stood peering with brimming eyes through the east window. She had young Tommy in her arms. Her husband's departing stride, the sudden slamming of the door, crashed against her ears with the numbing impact of a bullet.

The sun climbed with a poky, maddening indifference.

A cock crowed down in the bottoms somewhere and a wind sprang up and light rushed over the town in a golden floor, but no birds sang.

Inside Wyatt's room at the Cosmopolitan, Laura sat frozen as he buckled on his shell belts and checked the loads of his long-barreled pistols. He turned and for a moment looked mutely in her direction. Then he caught up a shotgun, pulled open the door and went off down the hall, leaving Laura listening to the diminishing pound of his boots.

Somewhere another door slammed shut.

Where were the Clantons?

Virgil and Morgan Earp were sighted walking slowly up Fourth between Allen and Fremont, both dressed in the black frock coats of gamblers. Then Wyatt was sighted cutting in from the left. His stride was brisk, his face expressionless. He carried a shotgun under one arm. The sun struck glints from the badge

189

that now and again was uncovered by his open coat.

Doc, in his room, heard Wyatt stomp down the hall. He was awake and sober, but still on his back, shoulders propped with pillows. He felt a vague curiosity as to what might have put Wyatt abroad so early. He told himself it was no skin off his nose but he could not put his strange uneasiness aside.

Six riders cut darkly over the rim of the mesa and came on without talk up Allen and north on Third and around into Fremont, entering the corral, where they got off their horses and hitched them.

Ike, spruced up in his cowboy best, stared around, looking over the situation. This O. K. Corral was a livery stable with open-air pens for the horses at the rear, that much of it extending no farther than an alley bisecting the block from east to west. North of the alley was an open yard. Fencing it across the Fourth Street end was the photo shop and studio of C. S. Fly. An assayer's office provided a wall on the Third Street side, and here for the moment both Clantons, the two McLowrys and Claibourne were standing. Wes Fuller had stepped over to the alley to look about for the Earps and make sure his friends were not surprised.

Meanwhile, on Fourth Street, Morgan and Virgil had been joined by Wyatt Morgan, attempting to strike a lighter note, remarked.

'You look like you've made up your mind to something. You're not aiming to call this deal off, I hope?'

'I guess,' Virgil winked, 'he's been wrasslin' with his conscience.'

Wyatt, peering over at the assayer's office, seeming to be grimly studying the door, did not bother to answer this badinage. He did, indeed, have a rather determined expression on his face, eyes half shut, wholly absorbed in whatever had hold of him. It was here that Doc, hurrying north off Allen, caught up with them, breathing heavily.

When he got back enough of his wind to speak, he said rather testily, 'A fine bunch you are, sneaking off with never a word. If Laura—'

'No sense,' Wyatt growled, 'you gettin' mixed up in a deal that was aimed primarily at me. Those rustlin' sons are after me, personal—an' after Virgil as chief upholder of the law around here. It's got nothing to do with you, Doc.'

'That's a hell of a thing for you to say to me!' Doc snarled, affronted.

He had some right to his outrage. Having spent most of the night sleeping off his jag, and no remembrance of Wyatt having come to his room, he would have remained totally unaware of what was impending if Laura hadn't burst into the room crying, 'Doc! Get up! They're all fixed to slaughter each other over at the O. K. Corral!'

191

'Who? What?' Doc stumbled from the bed, fighting to hold his balance while the room spun around him, and trying to think what he had done with his pistol.

'The McLowrys—the Clantons—'

'Doc, you can't!' Kate said, coming out of her chair. 'You can't hardly stand up!'

Doc squeezed his eyes shut, impatiently knuckling them. 'Get out of my way, woman.'

'No! I won't let you!' Glaring furiously at Laura, Kate cried, 'Can't you see he's too weak, too sick to stand up? Ain't you got no decency in you at all? Doc, you get back in that bed—'

He threw her hands off him. 'Be still! You and I, we don't matter—never have an' never will. Wyatt's chewed off too big a chunk this time, and what happens to him could affect the whole country, set things back twenty years. He's got to have help, no two ways about it.'

He got his gun rig buckled and shrugged into a gray coat, clapped on his hat and went reeling through the door, leaving Kate fuming at Laura.

The crisp morning air, on top of the shock Laura's words had given him, had by the time he reached Wyatt pretty well sobered him. Seeing him in that pearl gray suit and expensive headgear with a cane in his hand, you would hardly have guessed he'd just come off a bender. His color wasn't good and bags sagged beneath his eyes. He hadn't stopped to shave but there was a deadly aura about him that turned Wyatt thoughtful. After all, this bunch was after Doc, too; about the only friends the gambler had in this town were the Earps. He was not a man who made friends, not an easy man to know or like. But his word was good and if you had his allegiance you had it all the way.

'Get rid of that cane.' Wyatt passed him the shotgun. 'Stick this under your coat.' He said to the others, remembering Laura, 'We're going to do this different. Those boys are rustlers. Everybody knows it; there are enough counts against Ike to hang him twice over. There'll be no show of weapons. I intend to disarm and arrest the lot of them.'

His brothers grunted in astonishment. Doc said, 'You crazy?'

'Maybe. We'll pretty soon see.'

'And what about Jimmy?' Virgil said. 'You forgetting him?'

'I'm not forgetting a thing. We can't go after those boys on a personal basis. As officers our first loyalty is to the people of Tombstone—to the law itself. It's *law* we're trying to establish in this town. If responsible people make every issue personal we'll never have anything around here but anarchy.'

Morgan stared at Wyatt as though completely baffled. 'But you told them we'd meet them—'

'And so we will, but we'll do it as officers.'

'They'll never give up their guns,' Virgil said. 'It's either wipe us out or they're done, and they know it. You're asking—'

'We've got to try,' Wyatt said with finality.

'I've got a hunch,' Doc grinned with a wink and a chuckle, 'our righteous friend has been listening to a lady.' He saw the angry glint coming into Wyatt's eyes and said quickly, getting down to cases, 'That bunch—no matter what they proposed—ain't figuring to come out on the short end of this. They're going to have all the help they reckon to need.'

Morgan nodded soberly. Wyatt said, 'Let's get on with it.'

Cotton Wilson, standing with Wes Fuller in the alley, came onto the street, intercepting them. Fuller, ducking back, went hurrying off. Wilson said, 'You may have forgotten it, but I'm still sheriff and there's not going to be any gunplay while I'm able to prevent—'

'You figure you're able to, do you?' Wyatt looked him over, plainly skeptical. 'I recollect asking for your cooperation. Seems you had a hands-off policy in anything like to advantage your friends—'

'It's not a question of friendship.'

'You been hobnobbing with 'em.' Doc's cold eyes were as gray and hard as bullets.

'I been readin' 'em the riot act. They've seen the light.' His shifting glance whipped to Wyatt. 'You go starting a gunplay you're done around here.' He said, red-faced, 'I'll see you

194

strung up—'

'Talk's cheap,' Doc scoffed. 'I've heard the wind blow before.'

Cotton jerked away his angry eyes. 'Wyatt, Ike wants to talk.'

'Somebody sitting on his shirttail?'

'He'll do his talking over there. I can't blame him.'

'Of course you can't, Cotton—not and pocket his money. All right, I'll step over—'

'Don't be a fool!' Doc growled.

Morgan said with his face not over a foot from the sheriff: 'Do you take us for suckers? We know what's back of this. This whole crummy deal was ribbed up by Ike. They laid for Wyatt last night and got Jimmy. Now they're fixin' to wipe out the rest of us.'

'That's a goddam lie!' Wilson shouted.

Wyatt waved Virgil back. 'You've got a number of choices, Cotton. You can yank your iron now, or get on down there with your chums, or you can climb on a horse and start splittin' the breeze. And I'm telling you this in all kindness. The politics that's got you doubled over backwards don't make no real never-mind to me. What does matter to me is that this here locality has been under the Clanton heel long enough. We're arresting that bunch. Now get out of my way.'

He shoved past the livid sheriff and struck off up the street, the others spreading out till their advance occupied the riffled dust from walk to walk, Doc flanking Wyatt.

'I never reckoned,' Wyatt said, 'you were going to be in on this. I'm not sure if I could have gone through with it without you.'

Doc didn't answer, but under his breath he began softly to whistle.

*　　　*　　　*

Wes Fuller, back at the Corral, hurried into the wagon yard. 'They're comin'—all four of 'em!' He showed a wolfish grin. 'All three Earps an' Doc!'

'Then we've got 'em where we want 'em. Get that wagon pushed over against the entrance.'

He gestured at Ringo, Finn, the McLowrys and young Billy, who was actually nineteen, not the sixteen Wyatt imagined. Behind his youth he was as iron-nerved and reckless as the buck-toothed young hellion, Billy the Kid, whom he had adopted as his idol. He actually had more guts than the rest of this tribe all rolled into one. These five manhandled the wagon over to where Ike wanted it. As a matter of fact, this was a covered wagon, and it now pretty completely blocked the mouth of the Corral.

'Tom,' Ike said, 'you get inside of it. Take your rifle.'

'Goddam,' Tom growled, 'that ain't much cover.' And his brother, Frank, said, 'I don't

196

like it.'

'Who's runnin' this deal?' Ike said.

Tom, still grumbling, got into the wagon. 'That's our ace in the hole,' Ike said to the others. 'We'll draw their attention. All Tom's got to do is cut them sonofabitches down.'

Tom McLowry, then, behind his canvas, was the nearest man to the approaching officers.

Cotton Wilson, sprinting in from the alley, got Ike aside, unloaded his news, and ducked back toward Fremont. Ike and the rest of them deployed to take up positions with the adobe wall of the assayer's shack back of them. Now they could see the four approaching men fanned out across the street. Ringo said, 'I'll take care of Doc, personal.'

'You, Cotton,' Ike growled, 'git over there by them horses.'

'Jesus Christ!' Cotton snarled, 'I can't take part in this!'

'You'll take part. Git over there.'

The Earps and Doc were pretty close in, now, about twenty feet from the wagon-blocked entrance. They were now somewhat shadowed by those across-the-street buildings but, in all conscience, plain enough to be dropped by Tom McLowry where he hid inside the wagon.

All motion ceased. In this absolute quiet, Wyatt stepped into the full smash of the sun. 'Ike,' he shouted, 'you and your outfit are under arrest for the murder of James Earp.

197

Throw down your guns and walk out with your hands up.'

A floorboard skreaked inside the wagon. 'Hit the dirt!' Doc yelled.

Wyatt was already dropping but the consumptive gambler, on the extreme outside edge, was unable to bring his Greener into play without being as likely to nick friend as foe. Behind his canvas-and-wood barricade Tom McLowry's rifle sent the first report slambanging across that exploding quiet. The shot, with its ballooning burst of black power, gave away his hidey hole. Virgil and Morgan, opening up with their sixshooters, splintered the wagonbed and gophered several holes through the rickety sideboards.

Wyatt, scrambling up, plunged over the dust. The Clantons, ducking with his bullets whanging over them, allowed him to reach the corner of the assayer's shop. Morgan and Virgil, still in Doc's line of fire, prevented him from opening up with the shotgun. He was swearing like a muleskinner, cursing them and the Clantons impartially. Finn, Billy Clanton and Ringo made it too hot for Wyatt to quit his captured corner. Ringo, also furiously cursing, tried to get off a shot at Doc but was prevented by the squealing gyrations of the tied and frantic Clanton horses. Powdersmoke swirled its stink over everything, reducing visibility, adding nothing at all to the belligerents' accuracy and doubtless, with the churned-up dust, delaying the bloody finish by several hectic seconds.

Cotton Wilson, not far from Wyatt but still in the open, stood shaking in his boots as the battle got under way. Stampeded into a sudden run, he got into the pitching Clanton horses, scrambled aboard one and cut it loose. Ike Clanton, snarling, drove four shots into the sheriffs back. He might have wasted more if Ringo, furious, hadn't spun him around, pointing him at Doc's abruptly uncovered position.

It was easy, with that racket of shots bursting out, to imagine Virgil's wife Betty, left waiting and frightened in their home down the street, clutching their young son Tommy to her, perhaps lifting a tragic face in prayer.

Wyatt, pinned down behind his corner of the wall by the concentrated fire of Ringo, Billy and the gaunt Finn Clanton, heard the thump and whine of the lead flying past him. Trying for a look at something to shoot at, he was nearly blinded by a spattering barrage of dust and adobe grit.

Doc saw him reel back. Saw Tom McLowry, abandoning both his cover and rifle, break from the sheeted wagon and, with a sixshooter shoved forgotten in the waistband of his pants, make a desperate dash for the terrified horses which had thus far kept Doc from flanking the main position. Morgan, attempting to do just that, raced into Fremont Street. Finn Clanton, diving forward, scuttled under the wagon, came up on one knee, and triggering furiously, cut Morgan down.

Both Wyatt and Virgil turned their guns on the now exposed Finn. Struck, arms flopping, Finn's hatless head went through the spokes of a wheel. His knees jerked up and then unfolded limply.

Billy Claibourne, sprinting out from his stance somewhat off to one side, started emptying his gun in the direction of Virgil, loosing three wild shots before, panicking, he dashed for the protection of Fly's photographic shop. Wyatt, Doc observed, was under fire from Billy Clanton and Frank McLowry. In the midst of this Wyatt, coming away from his wall in a zigzagging crouch, opened up with both pistols, doubling McLowry who clutched frantically at his belly and dived forward onto his face. Morgan Earp, though wounded and down in the dust, tried to drop Tom McLowry before Tom reached the horses.

Ike Clanton, a sixshooter hanging wholly useless from his fist, stood upright, staring glassy-eyed at the carnage round him until the vision of Claibourne's desertion and Frank McLowry's shriek of anguish as he grabbed both hands to his belly and fell unlocked him from his petrified stance. Pumping frozen legs into a spasm of activity big Ike, loudly yelling for mercy, charged toward Wyatt with both fists over his head.

'You sonofabitch!' Ringo snarled, jerking his gun up. Young Billy, slamming into the gunslinger's shoulder, upset his aim. Staggered by this deliberate collision Ringo was forced to forgo his intention, putting all his anger into keeping his feet.

Wyatt, in all the uproar and confusion, someway managed to keep his head and, with the yelling Ike boiling out of the powder fog practically upon him—almost running him down—had the astonishing forbearance not to put a slug through him. What he did as Ike grabbed hold of him, babbling hysterically not to be killed, was to shake the man off. 'This fight's commenced,' he snarled, livid with fury. 'Get to fighting or get out of my way!'

Fly's studio wasn't ten jumps away and Ike barreled through the door Billy Claibourne shoved open for him.

But there was nothing of the coward about young Billy Clanton, already wounded and with blood running out of him. Nicked by Wyatt and with his right arm broken by a bullet from Virgil, he let go of his pistol, grabbed it into his left hand and looked for somebody to use it on.

Meanwhile Doc, in a cursing splutter of impatience at being so long compelled to the role of an observer, saw Tom McLowry, among the horses, commence to bang away at Wyatt. Wyatt creased one of the plunging animals; this and another snapped their reins and departed, leaving McLowry in the windy open.

Doc lost no time in throwing down on him. Swinging up his shotgun he emptied both barrels. For a moment it appeared that he had missed completely. McLowry, leaping past the corner of the corral, made off down Fremont at a skittering gallop. But on his seventh or eighth leap he came apart in the middle and fell all spraddled out, dead enough to skin.

Billy Clanton, badly bleeding but upright and paying no attention to the bullets winging past him, with the gun in his left hand shot Town Marshal Virgil in the thigh, knocking him down. Before Billy could thumb back his hammer again Morgan, also bleeding from a bullet in his right shoulder, came out of the twists of dust and powdersmoke and flung Billy back with a slug through the chest.

Doc, throwing his shotgun away, snatched out his nickel-plated Colt .45. Inside Fly's photo shop Claibourne and Ike now went into action, taking the officers from the rear. Morgan, whirling, was smashed back and down.

Doc drove two slugs through the nearest window. The rear door flew open and Ike, legs pistoning, came out with the gigantic jumps of a rabbit. Doc made two more tries but Ike, really heating his axles, loped off out of range and disappeared inside the barn. With but one bean left in the cylinder, Doc faced around and found young Clanton, still upright and dangerous, sidling along the wall toward the relative cover of the corner Wyatt, just moments ago, had abandoned. And Frank McLowry, incredibly up again after his collapse from Wyatt's belly shot, was moving with astounding fortitude and courage in the same direction, barelipped and snarling, shooting as he went.

Wyatt put a slug through Billy's hips, nailing him in his tracks, but Frank was still on his way toward the street. His gun was up and he was looking straight at Doc, grinning like a damned hyena.

'Gotcha this time!' he croaked with the blood frothing down his chin.

'All you've got is hell,' Doc sneered and, twisting, drawing himself to the lanky full height of a dueler's stance, he squeezed off a shot at the same time Frank did. McLowry's slug scraped a streak of leather off Doc's holster, but the gambler's bullet—the last in his gun—went through Frank's heart. Almost simultaneously Morgan Earp, sprawled and bloody in the dust of the road, put a bullet through Frank's forehead. This time, when he dropped, he stayed down, completely motionless.

Young Billy, with his chin on his chest and back slumped now against the base of the wall, was still trying to get off another shot.

Mumbling or muttering—some said later he was praying for just enough strength to do it—he kept desperately trying to bring his gun into line with Wyatt who, holding his fire, continued solemnly to watch him. Doc threw down on Billy Claibourne, now in full flight in the wake of Ike Clanton, but the hammer clicked emptily. Doc had no bullets left.

Billy Clanton finally toppled forward into the dust.

Witnesses have said that, from the time Tom McLowry got off the first shot until the gun dropped out of young Billy's lifeless hand, not over thirty seconds elapsed. The most conservative estimates place the duration of the battle at something under one minute.

Ike Clanton and Claibourne fled like the big-mouthed cowards they were. Both McLowrys, Billy Clanton and Cotton Wilson had gone to their rewards. The town came cautiously out of hiding and those who had been near enough to witness the action began to converge on the scene with diverse exclamations, more than a few of them shaking their heads and feeling inexpressibly thankful to be alive and no worse off than they were.

The power of the Clantons was forever ended. Virgil, Doc and Morgan were wounded. Doc had a bullet burn across his back. Morgan had a bullet hole through his right shoulder. Virgil, chief of the town's law enforcement officers, twice wounded, suffered most from the slug young Clanton had driven into his thigh. Only Doc and Wyatt, who had come through the fight unscathed, were able to carry on.

Fortunately, in addition to those coming to view the shambles, a number of Clum's vigilantes arrived to take over the policing of the town, fearing reprisals by others of the cow crowd. Announcing that Virgil and his deputies had their complete support, Clum's men mounted a twenty-four-hour guard to stand off any attempts against the wounded officers, who were promptly removed to Virgil's home.

With the gunshots from the battle crashing around their ears, Kate and Laura, still in Doc's room at the Cosmopolitan, had been dying a dozen deaths of their own, Laura with her eyes shut, Kate with her head pushed against Laura's shoulder. The reports, though muffled by distance, were all too plain. At last Kate jumped up. 'I can't stand it!' she cried, beside herself, and rushed from the room, Laura hastening after her.

Doc, as he parted from Wyatt at the corner of Fourth, growled, 'What in seven hells did you let Ike get away for?'

'He wouldn't draw,' Wyatt said. 'Did you think I would gun him down in cold blood?'

Right after Doc left him Wyatt heard the hoofbeats of a hard-running team and saw the Clanton wagon coming. He stepped back on the walk but Mrs. Clanton, recognizing him, flung back on the reins and pulled the lathered broncs up. The old lady and the marshal exchanged a long look. Her eyes fell away from him. With an inarticulate cry, she snatched up the reins and drove on.

There was nothing Wyatt could have said to her, but he regretted it deeply. Too, he wanted to go over to Virgil's place and see how his brothers were getting along; indeed, he had been intending to do this when he'd taken leave of Doc. But it came over him now that his first duty, after all, was to the town and the law whose badge he wore. With a weary sigh, he reckoned he had better go back to the office.

*   *   *

Doc, almost immediately after leaving the marshal's company, encountered Kate and Laura hurrying toward the O. K. Corral. 'Thank God!' Kate cried, trying to fling herself into his arms. The gambler caught her wrists and held her away from him. She started to fly into a rage and then, her face went white, still and startled. She knew how intensely he disliked public displays but she could not keep her concern from showing. 'You've been shot!' she gasped. 'My God—is it bad, Doc?'

'It's nothing but a scratch,' he said, embarrassed and trying to edge around Laura.

'If you've got to talk let's do it someplace else.'

'Now you stand right there,' Kate snapped, getting riled again. 'If you're hurt, that's one thing. If you ain't—'

Doc said to Laura, 'Wyatt's all right. I think he's gone over to Virgil's. Virg and Morgan—'

'You listen to me!' Kate shouted. 'If you're able to stand here and gab, you can travel. You promised we were going to Bisbee today and I'm not forgettin' it. You go over to that saloon and get in some game we'll never get out of here! This town's . . .'

Laura left them wrangling and moved on up the street. She felt sorry for Kate, but most of Kate's troubles came out of her own nature, her own impatience and foolishness, her own ungovernable rages. Doc wasn't a man who could be handled with belligerence.

She was tremendously relieved to learn that Wyatt had not been hurt. She loved him deeply—she guessed she always would—but she knew him as well as anyone could and was astute enough to see that he would not give up the star now. She tried to analyze her feelings, to study her needs, to discover if there were areas of common interest strong enough to bridge the disparity in their relations.

It was while she was doing this, searching her soul, that she rounded the corner and came abruptly upon him.

Wyatt's eyes lit up. 'Laura! My dear!'

She gave him her hands. She saw his dismay

when she refused to come into his arms, saw the bleakness enter his expression again and turn his face unreadable.

'Don't,' she whispered. 'Don't say it, Wyatt. I'll always love you but we've come as close to each other as we can. My things are packed, I'm leaving this noon.'

*   *   *

Doc, when Wyatt reached the hotel, was standing by Wyatt's saddled horse, alone and not looking at all his usual immaculate and rather jaunty self.

Stepping over to his horse, Wyatt tightened the cinches. The street seemed strangely deserted, strangely drab despite the bright sunlight and a freshening breeze.

'So you're finally making it to California,' Doc said.

Wyatt frowned into space for a while. 'No. I reckon not, Doc.' He sighed. 'I guess I'm just too set in my ways to get properly interested in a bunch of dumb cows.' He laughed shortly, without mirth.

'You're staying here?'

'I'll stay till Virgil gets back on his feet. How about you?'

Doc stared out across the street. 'Staying here, with me, is mostly a matter of pride, or maybe damnfool stubbornness. It might be that, like you, I've got into a rut—but it suits

208

me. I'm comfortable.' He looked very determined. Then he got to coughing.

Wyatt watched him cover his mouth with a handkerchief.

'You ought to go up to that hospital in Denver.'

Doc glanced at the handkerchief and put it away. 'And you ought to take Laura and head for California.'

'It wouldn't work,' Wyatt said. 'We both know it.'

Both men stood awkwardly silent for a space.

Then Doc, straightening his coat, said, 'Let's go have a drink.'